TOP SECRET GRAPHICA MYSTERIES

CASEBOOK: THE BERMUDA TRIANGLE

Script by Justine and Ron Fontes

Layouts and Designs by Ron Fontes

Skyview Books™

an imprint of

WINDMILL BOOKS™

New York

Published in 2010 by Windmill Books, LLC
303 Park Avenue South, Suite # 1280
New York, NY 10010-3657

CREDITS:
Script by Justine and Ron Fontes
Layouts and designs by Ron Fontes
Art by Planman, Ltd.

Publisher Cataloging in Publication

Fontes, Justine
       Casebook--the Bermuda Triangle. – School and library ed. / script by Justine and Ron Fontes; layouts and designs by Ron Fontes; art by Planman, Ltd.
p.   cm. – (Top secret graphica mysteries)
Summary: Edward Icarus Stein, nicknamed "Einstein," and his friends use their virtual visors to investigate some of the mysterious happenings in the Bermuda Triangle.
ISBN 978-1-60754-591-0 – ISBN 978-1-60754-592-7 (pbk.)
ISBN 978-1-60754-593-4 (6-pack)
       1.   Bermuda Triangle—Juvenile fiction   2. Graphic novels   [1. Bermuda Triangle—Fiction   2. Time travel—Fiction   3. Graphic novels]   I. Fontes, Ron   II. Title   III. Title: Bermuda Triangle   IV. Series
       741.5/973—dc22

Manufactured in the United States of America

CONTENTS

WELCOME TO THE WINDMILL BAKERY   PAGE 4

E. I. STEIN'S CASEBOOK   PAGE 7

FACT FILE   PAGE 44

FIND OUT FOR YOURSELF   PAGE 47

WEB SITES   PAGE 48

ABOUT THE AUTHOR/ARTIST   PAGE 48

Welcome to the Windmill Bakery

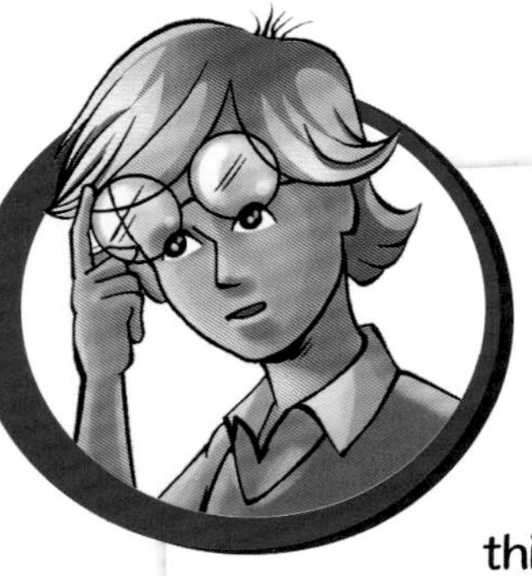

Edward Icarus Stein is known as "Einstein" because of his initials "E.I." and his last name, and because he loves science the way fanatical fans love sports. Einstein dedicates his waking hours to observing as much as he can of all the strange things just beyond human knowledge, because "that's the discovery zone," as he calls it. Einstein aspires to nothing less than living up to his nickname and coming up with a truly groundbreaking scientific discovery. So far this brilliant seventh grader's best invention is the Virtual Visors he and his friends use to explore strange phenomena. Einstein's parents own the local bakery where the friends meet.

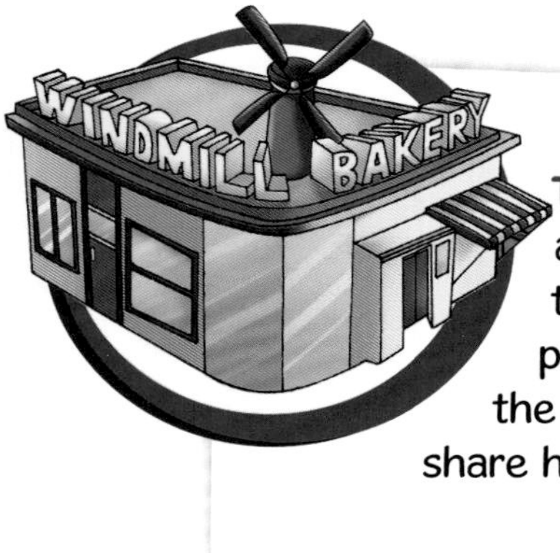
WINDMILL BAKERY

The Windmill Bakery is a cozy place where friends and neighbors buy homemade goodies to go or to eat on the premises. Einstein's kindhearted parents make everyone feel welcome, especially the friends who understand their exceptional son and share his appetite for discovery!

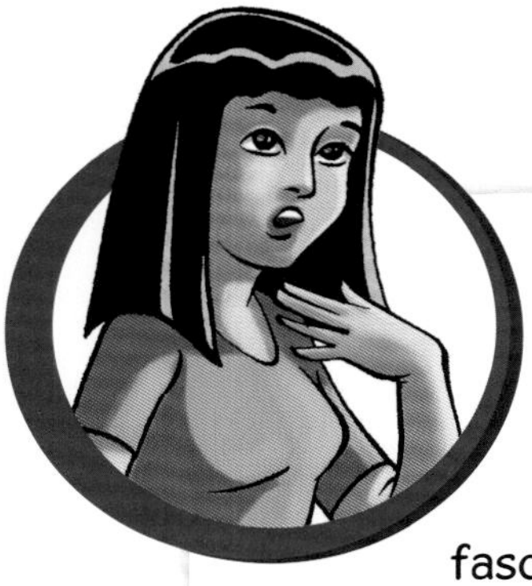

"Spacey Tracy" Lee saw a UFO when she was seven. Her parents tried to dismiss the incident as a "waking dream." But Tracy knew what she saw and it inspired her to investigate the UFO phenomenon. The more she learned, the more fascinated she became. She earned her nickname by constantly talking about UFOs. Tracy hopes to become a reporter when she grows up so she can continue to explore the unknown. A straight-A student, Tracy enjoys swimming, gymnastics, and playing the cello. Now that she's "more mature" and hoping to lose the silly nickname, Tracy shares the experience that changed her life forever only with her Virtual Visor buddies.

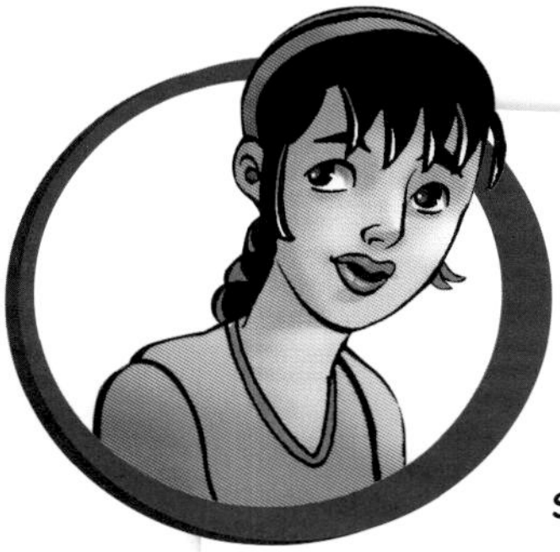

Clarita Gonzales knows that Indiana Jones and Lara Croft aren't real people, but that doesn't stop this seventh grader from wanting to be an adventurous archaeologist. Clarita's parents will support any path she chooses, as long as she gets a good education. Unfortunately, school isn't her strong point. During most classes, Clarita's mind wanders to, as she puts it, "more exciting places—like Atlantis!" A tomboy thanks to her three older brothers and one younger brother, Clarita is a great soccer player and is also into martial arts. Her interest in archaeology extends to architecture, artifacts, cooking, and all forms of culture. (Clarita would have a crush on Einstein if he wasn't "such a bookworm")!

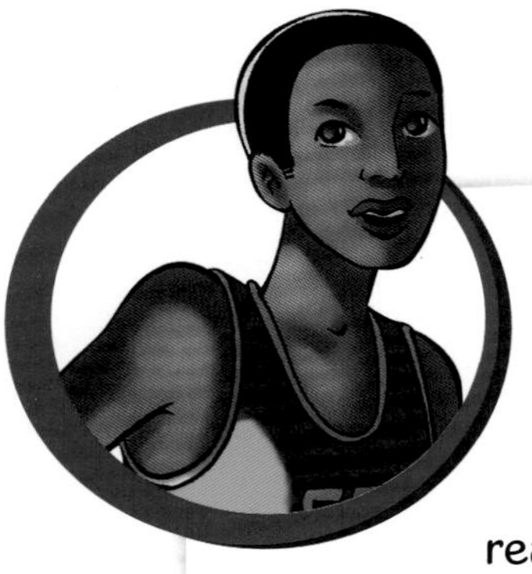

"Freaky Frank" Phillips earned his nickname because of his uncanny ability to use his "extra senses," a "gift" he inherited from his grandma. Though this eighth grader can't predict the winners of the next SUPERBOWL (or, he admits, "anything really useful"), Frank "knows" when someone is lying or otherwise up to no good. He gets "warnings" before trouble strikes. And sometimes he "sees things that aren't there"—at least to those less sensitive to things like auras and ghosts. Frank isn't sure what he wants to be when he grows up. He enjoys keeping tropical fish and does well in every subject, except math. "Numbers make my head hurt," Frank confesses. Frank spends lots of time with his family and his fish, but he's always up for an adventure with his friends.

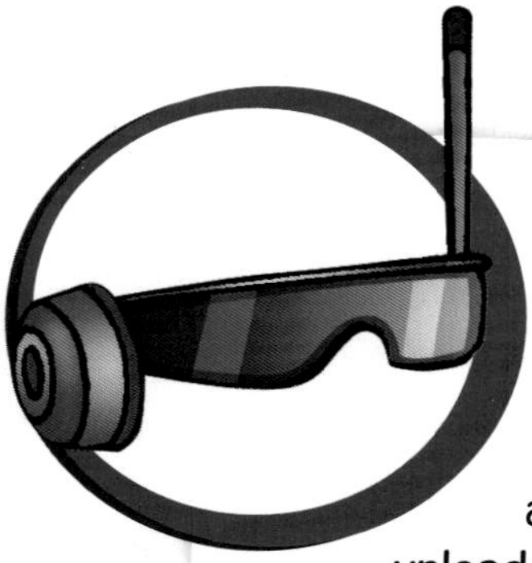

The Virtual Visors allow Einstein, Frank, Clarita, and Tracy to pursue their taste for adventure well beyond the boundaries of the bakery. Thanks to Einstein's brilliant software, the visors can simulate all kinds of locations and experiences based on the uploaded facts. Once inside the program, the visors become invisible. When danger gets too intense, the kids can always touch their Virtual Visors to return to the bakery. Sometimes the kids explore in the real world without the visors. But more often they use these devices to explore the mysteries and phenomena that intrigue each member of the group. The Virtual Visors are the ultimate virtual reality research tool, even though you never know what quirky things might happen thanks to Einstein's "Random Adventure Program."

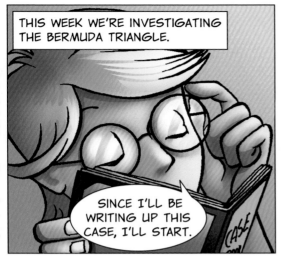

THIS WEEK WE'RE INVESTIGATING THE BERMUDA TRIANGLE.

SINCE I'LL BE WRITING UP THIS CASE, I'LL START.

AT THE BEGINNING, PLEASE, FOR THOSE OF US WHO *AREN'T* GENIUSES.

THE BERMUDA TRIANGLE CONNECTS FLORIDA, PUERTO RICO, AND BERMUDA.

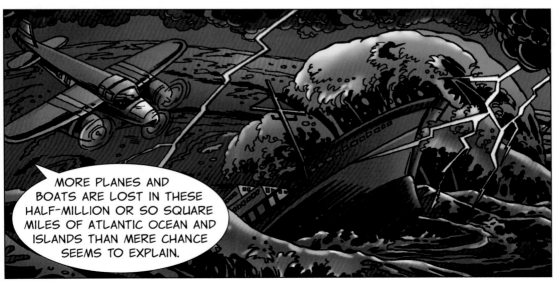

MORE PLANES AND BOATS ARE LOST IN THESE HALF-MILLION OR SO SQUARE MILES OF ATLANTIC OCEAN AND ISLANDS THAN MERE CHANCE SEEMS TO EXPLAIN.

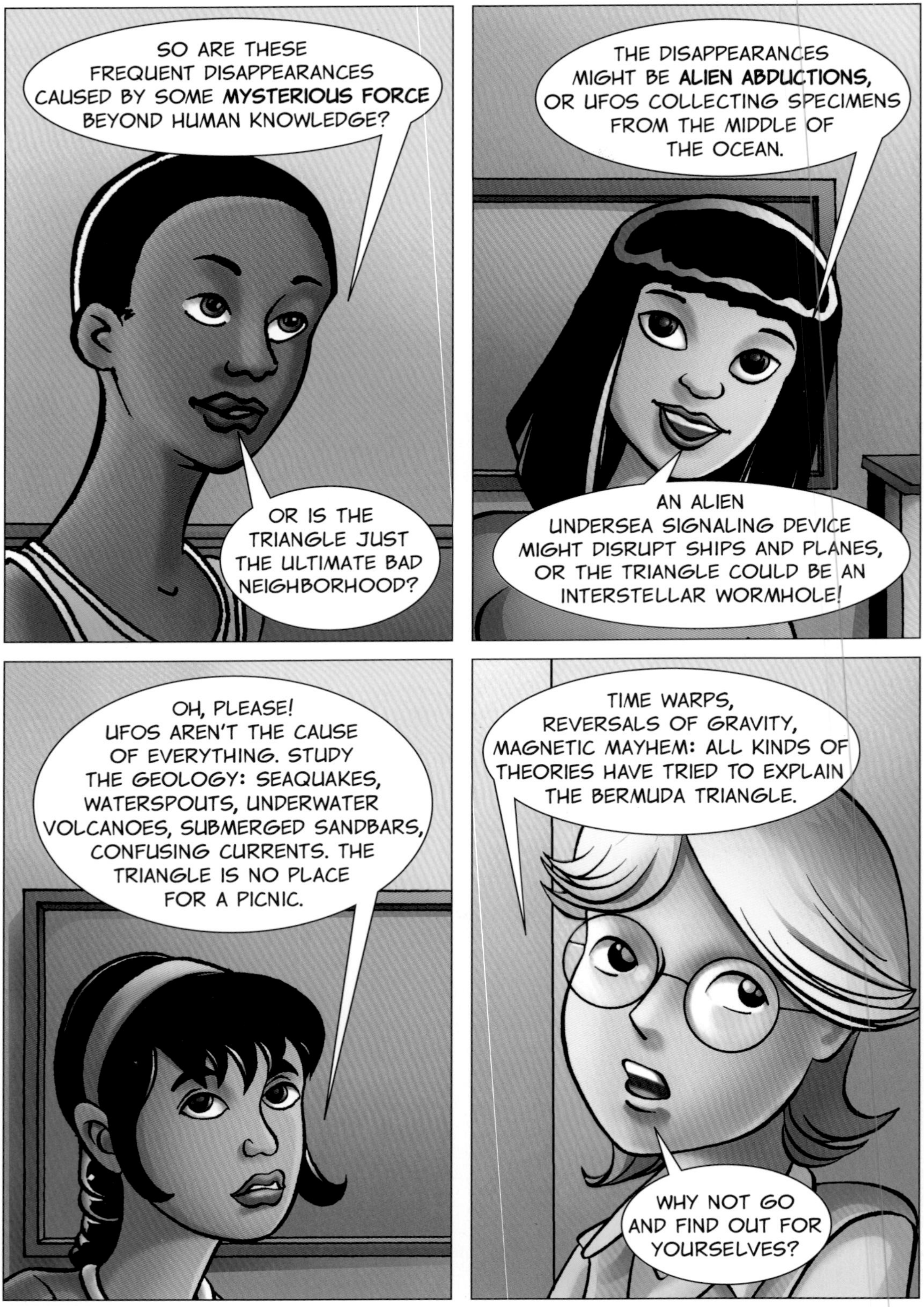
SO ARE THESE FREQUENT DISAPPEARANCES CAUSED BY SOME **MYSTERIOUS FORCE** BEYOND HUMAN KNOWLEDGE?
OR IS THE TRIANGLE JUST THE ULTIMATE BAD NEIGHBORHOOD?
THE DISAPPEARANCES MIGHT BE **ALIEN ABDUCTIONS,** OR UFOS COLLECTING SPECIMENS FROM THE MIDDLE OF THE OCEAN.
AN ALIEN UNDERSEA SIGNALING DEVICE MIGHT DISRUPT SHIPS AND PLANES, OR THE TRIANGLE COULD BE AN INTERSTELLAR WORMHOLE!
OH, PLEASE! UFOS AREN'T THE CAUSE OF EVERYTHING. STUDY THE GEOLOGY: SEAQUAKES, WATERSPOUTS, UNDERWATER VOLCANOES, SUBMERGED SANDBARS, CONFUSING CURRENTS. THE TRIANGLE IS NO PLACE FOR A PICNIC.
TIME WARPS, REVERSALS OF GRAVITY, MAGNETIC MAYHEM: ALL KINDS OF THEORIES HAVE TRIED TO EXPLAIN THE BERMUDA TRIANGLE.
WHY NOT GO AND FIND OUT FOR YOURSELVES?

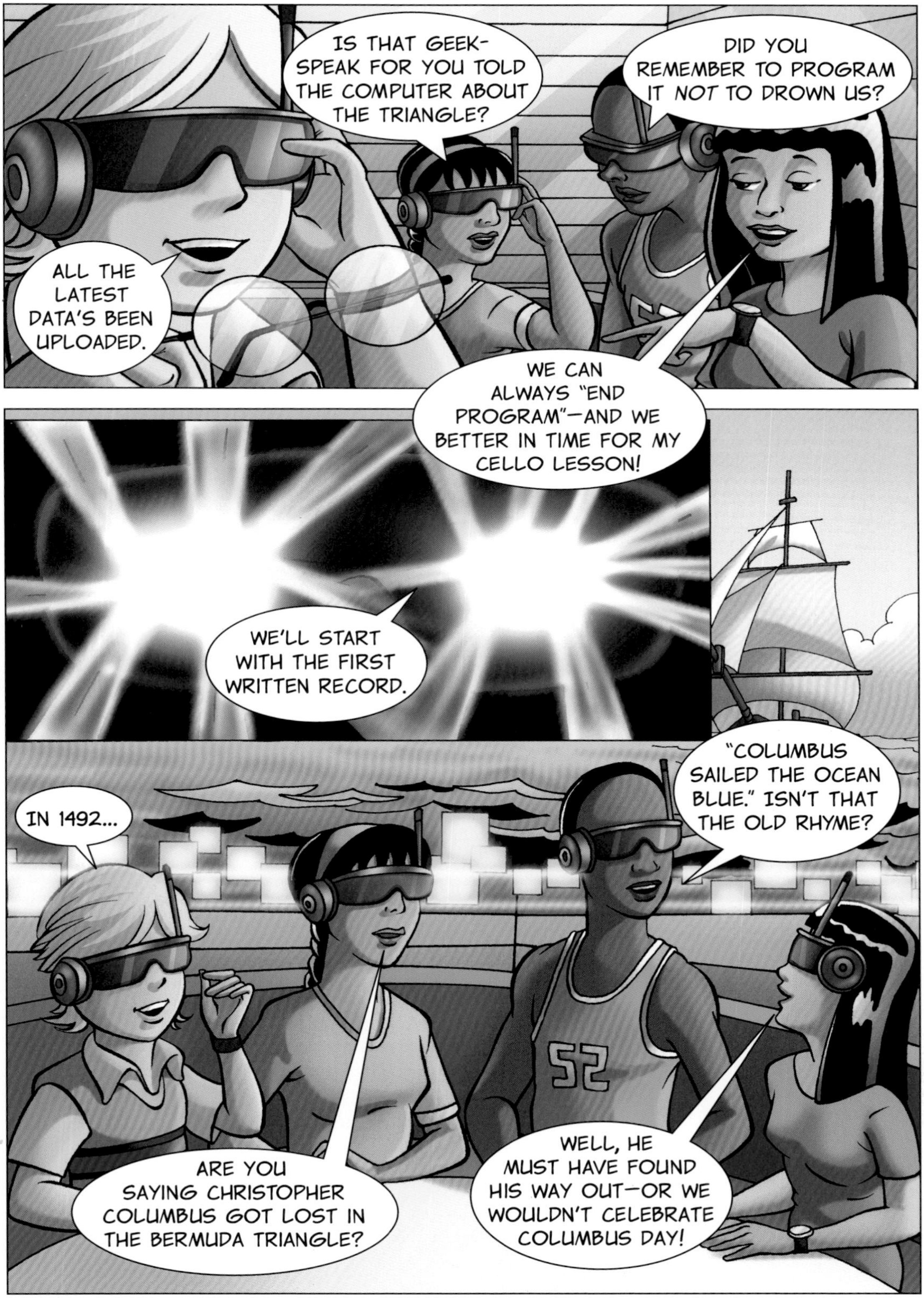
IS THAT GEEK-SPEAK FOR YOU TOLD THE COMPUTER ABOUT THE TRIANGLE?
DID YOU REMEMBER TO PROGRAM IT *NOT* TO DROWN US?
ALL THE LATEST DATA'S BEEN UPLOADED.
WE CAN ALWAYS "END PROGRAM"—AND WE BETTER IN TIME FOR MY CELLO LESSON!
WE'LL START WITH THE FIRST WRITTEN RECORD.
IN 1492...
"COLUMBUS SAILED THE OCEAN BLUE." ISN'T THAT THE OLD RHYME?
ARE YOU SAYING CHRISTOPHER COLUMBUS GOT LOST IN THE BERMUDA TRIANGLE?
WELL, HE MUST HAVE FOUND HIS WAY OUT—OR WE WOULDN'T CELEBRATE COLUMBUS DAY!

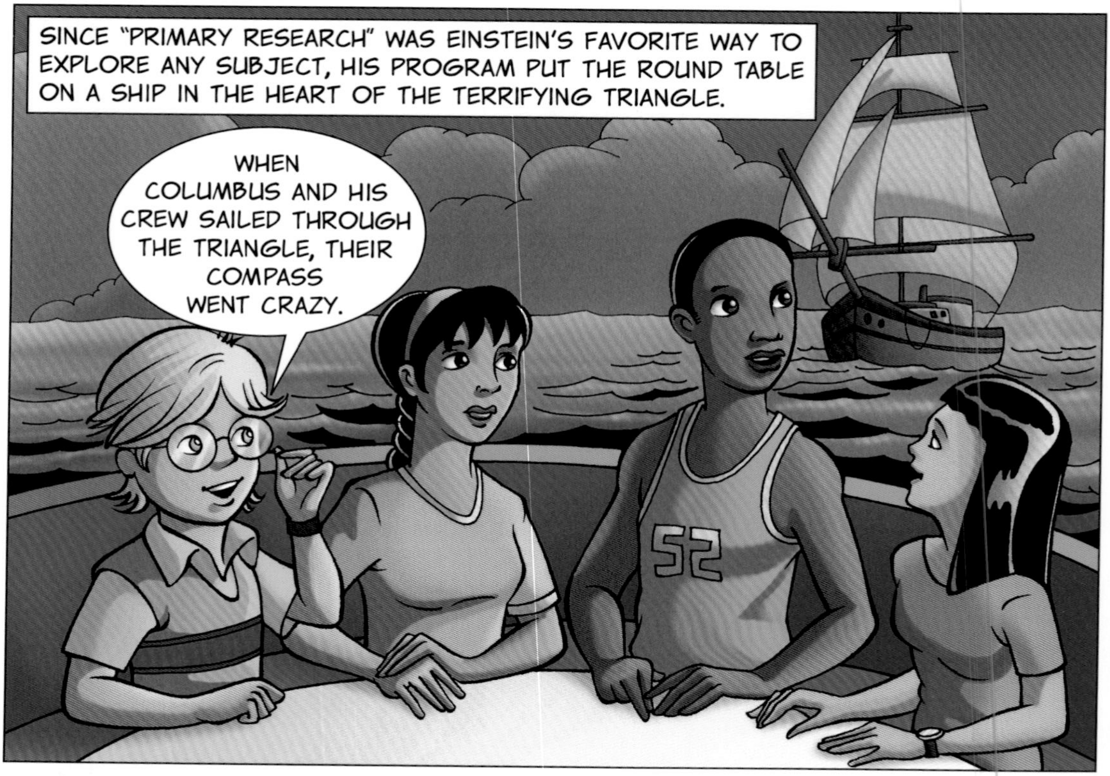
SINCE "PRIMARY RESEARCH" WAS EINSTEIN'S FAVORITE WAY TO EXPLORE ANY SUBJECT, HIS PROGRAM PUT THE ROUND TABLE ON A SHIP IN THE HEART OF THE TERRIFYING TRIANGLE.
WHEN COLUMBUS AND HIS CREW SAILED THROUGH THE TRIANGLE, THEIR COMPASS WENT CRAZY.
52

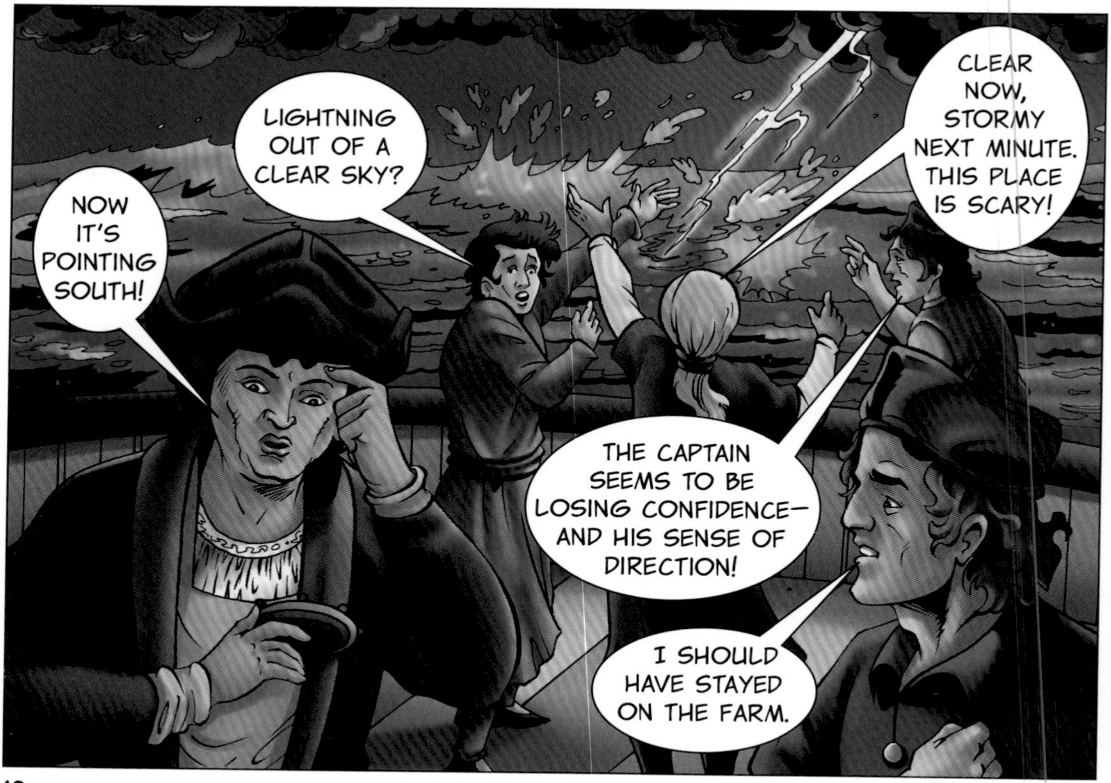
NOW IT'S POINTING SOUTH!
LIGHTNING OUT OF A CLEAR SKY?
CLEAR NOW, STORMY NEXT MINUTE. THIS PLACE IS SCARY!
THE CAPTAIN SEEMS TO BE LOSING CONFIDENCE— AND HIS SENSE OF DIRECTION!
I SHOULD HAVE STAYED ON THE FARM.

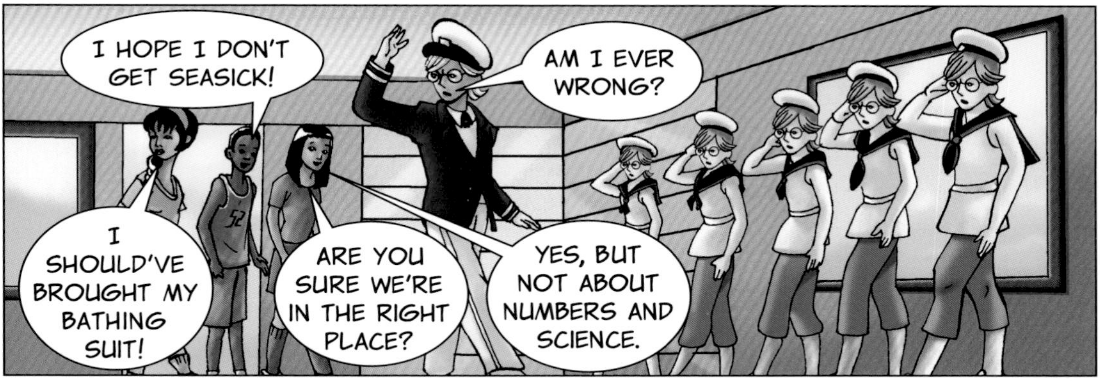
I HOPE I DON'T GET SEASICK!
I SHOULD'VE BROUGHT MY BATHING SUIT!
ARE YOU SURE WE'RE IN THE RIGHT PLACE?
AM I EVER WRONG?
YES, BUT NOT ABOUT NUMBERS AND SCIENCE.

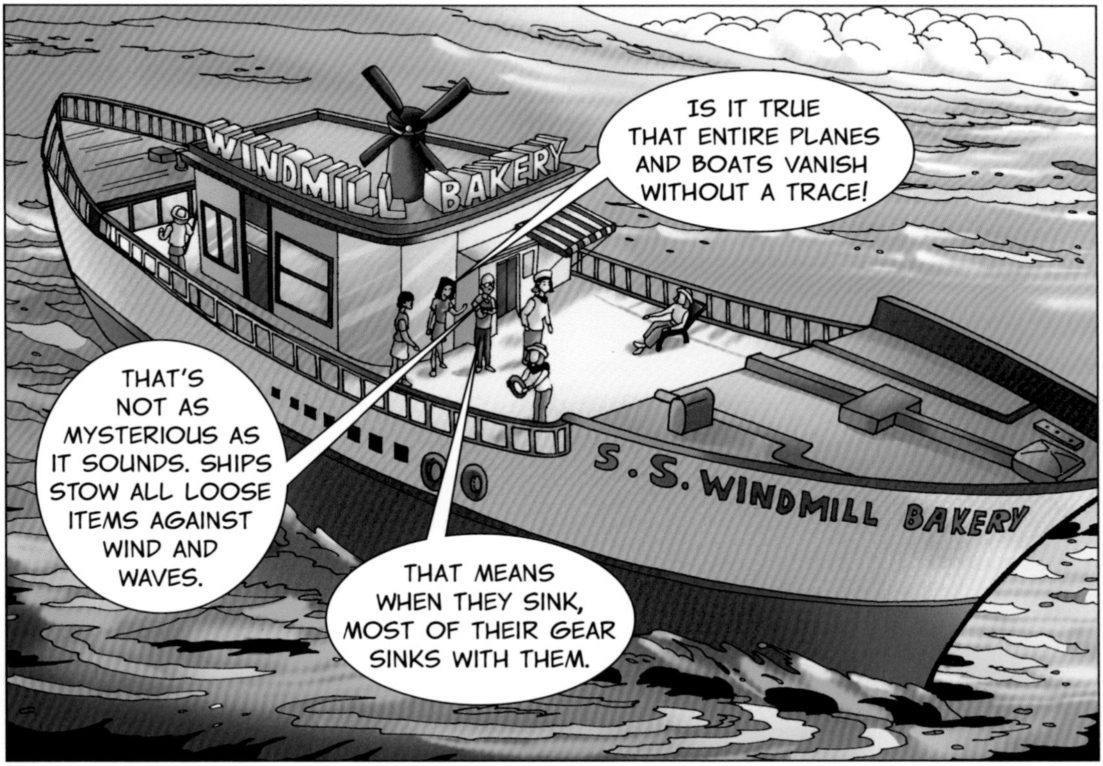
WINDMILL BAKERY
IS IT TRUE THAT ENTIRE PLANES AND BOATS VANISH WITHOUT A TRACE!
THAT'S NOT AS MYSTERIOUS AS IT SOUNDS. SHIPS STOW ALL LOOSE ITEMS AGAINST WIND AND WAVES.
THAT MEANS WHEN THEY SINK, MOST OF THEIR GEAR SINKS WITH THEM.
S.S. WINDMILL BAKERY

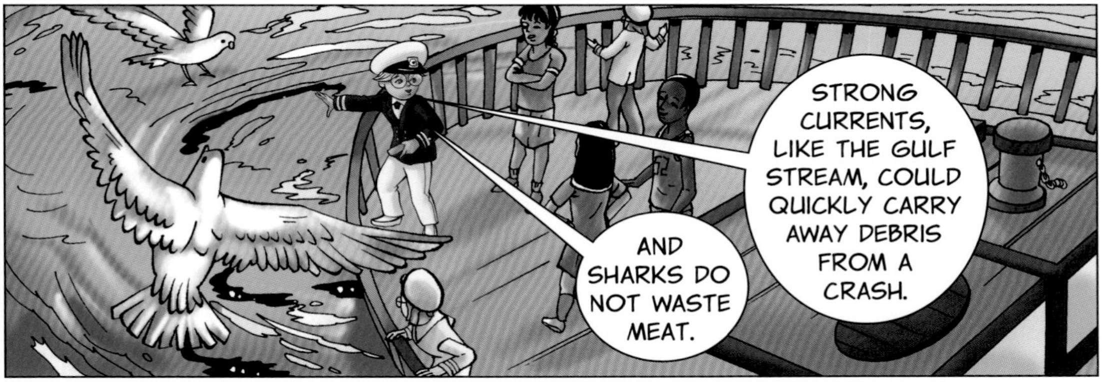
STRONG CURRENTS, LIKE THE GULF STREAM, COULD QUICKLY CARRY AWAY DEBRIS FROM A CRASH.
AND SHARKS DO NOT WASTE MEAT.

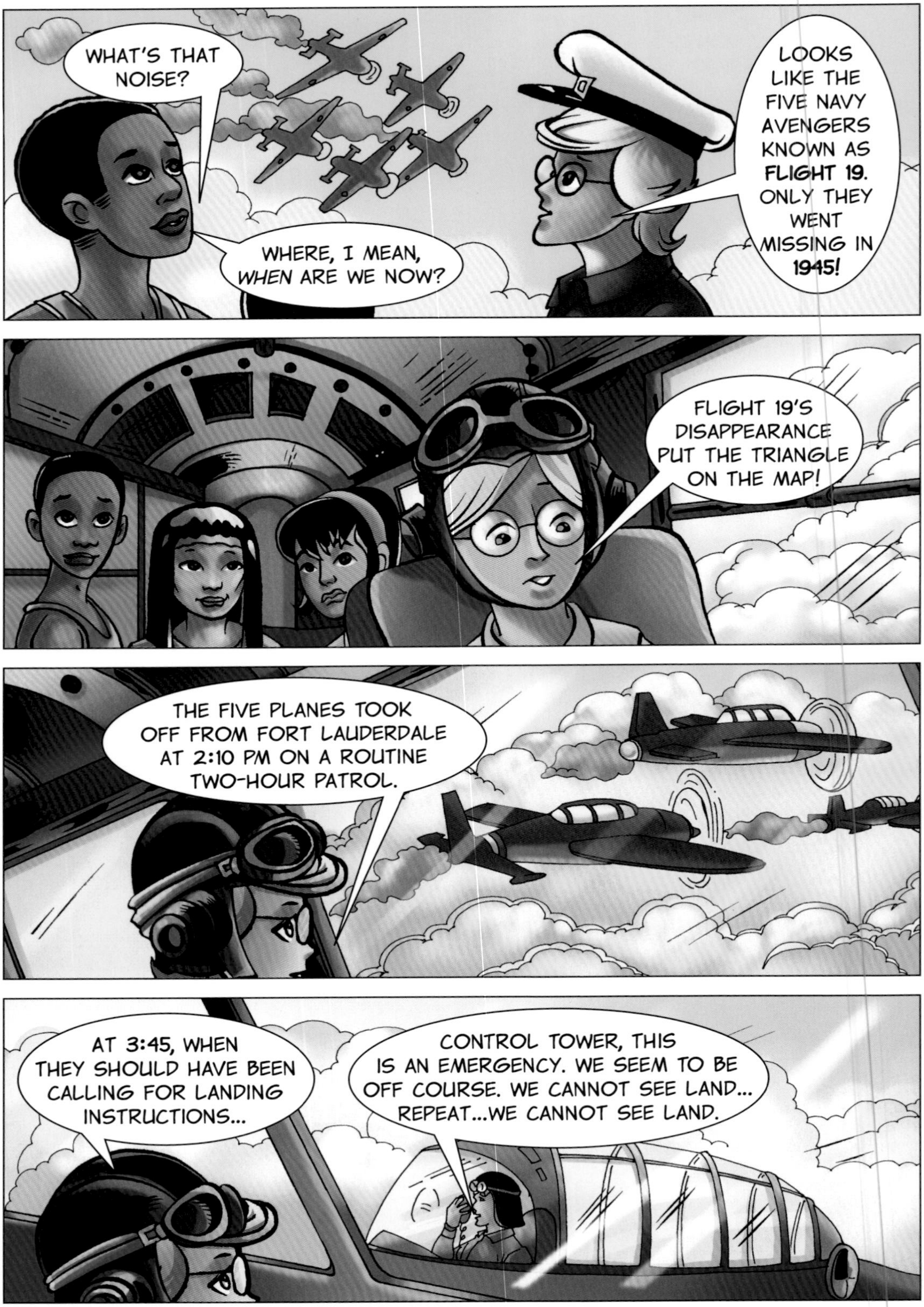
WHAT'S THAT NOISE?
WHERE, I MEAN, WHEN ARE WE NOW?
LOOKS LIKE THE FIVE NAVY AVENGERS KNOWN AS FLIGHT 19. ONLY THEY WENT MISSING IN 1945!
FLIGHT 19'S DISAPPEARANCE PUT THE TRIANGLE ON THE MAP!
THE FIVE PLANES TOOK OFF FROM FORT LAUDERDALE AT 2:10 PM ON A ROUTINE TWO-HOUR PATROL.
AT 3:45, WHEN THEY SHOULD HAVE BEEN CALLING FOR LANDING INSTRUCTIONS...
CONTROL TOWER, THIS IS AN EMERGENCY. WE SEEM TO BE OFF COURSE. WE CANNOT SEE LAND... REPEAT...WE CANNOT SEE LAND.

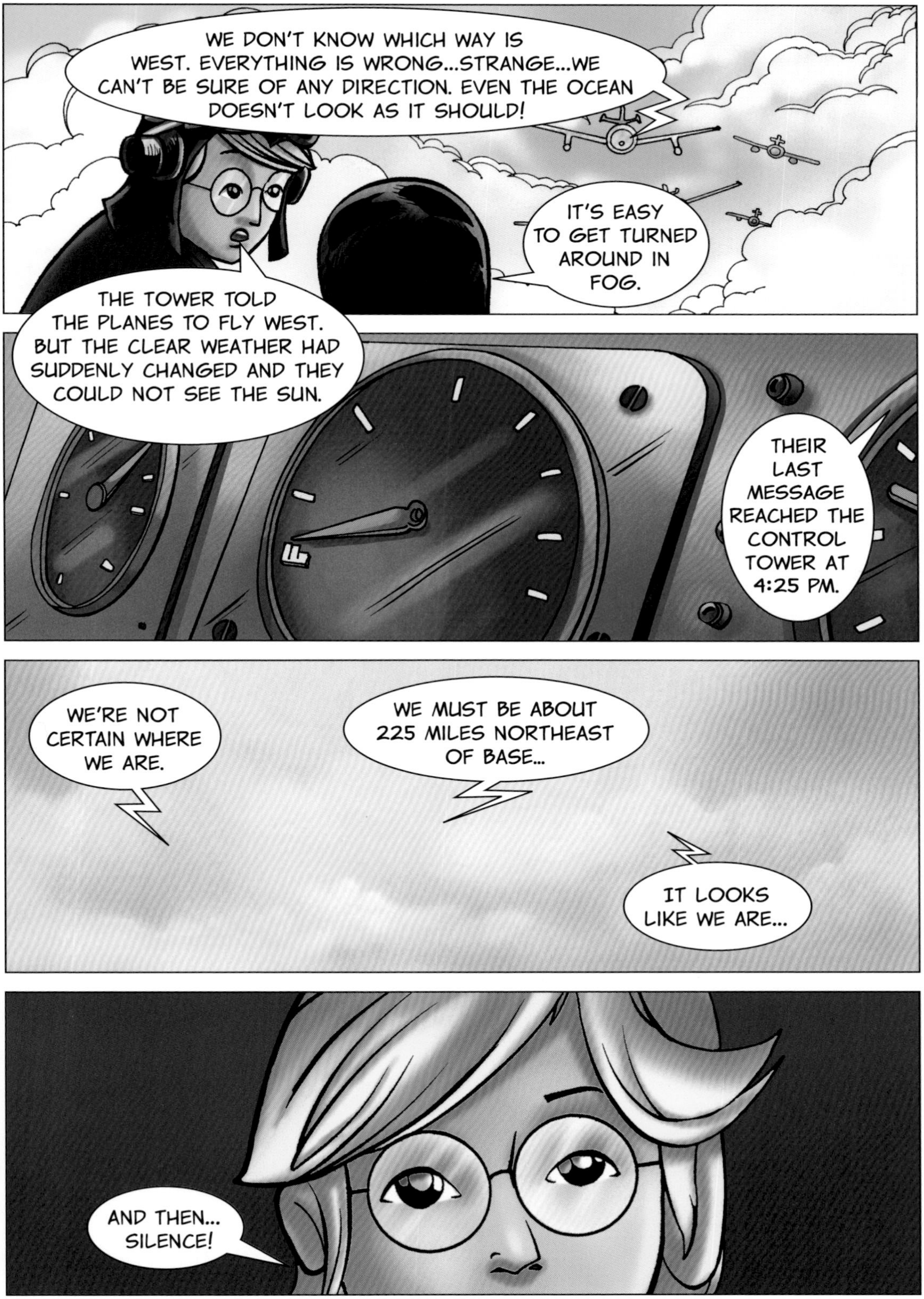
WE DON'T KNOW WHICH WAY IS WEST. EVERYTHING IS WRONG...STRANGE...WE CAN'T BE SURE OF ANY DIRECTION. EVEN THE OCEAN DOESN'T LOOK AS IT SHOULD!
IT'S EASY TO GET TURNED AROUND IN FOG.
THE TOWER TOLD THE PLANES TO FLY WEST. BUT THE CLEAR WEATHER HAD SUDDENLY CHANGED AND THEY COULD NOT SEE THE SUN.
THEIR LAST MESSAGE REACHED THE CONTROL TOWER AT 4:25 PM.
WE'RE NOT CERTAIN WHERE WE ARE.
WE MUST BE ABOUT 225 MILES NORTHEAST OF BASE...
IT LOOKS LIKE WE ARE...
AND THEN... SILENCE!

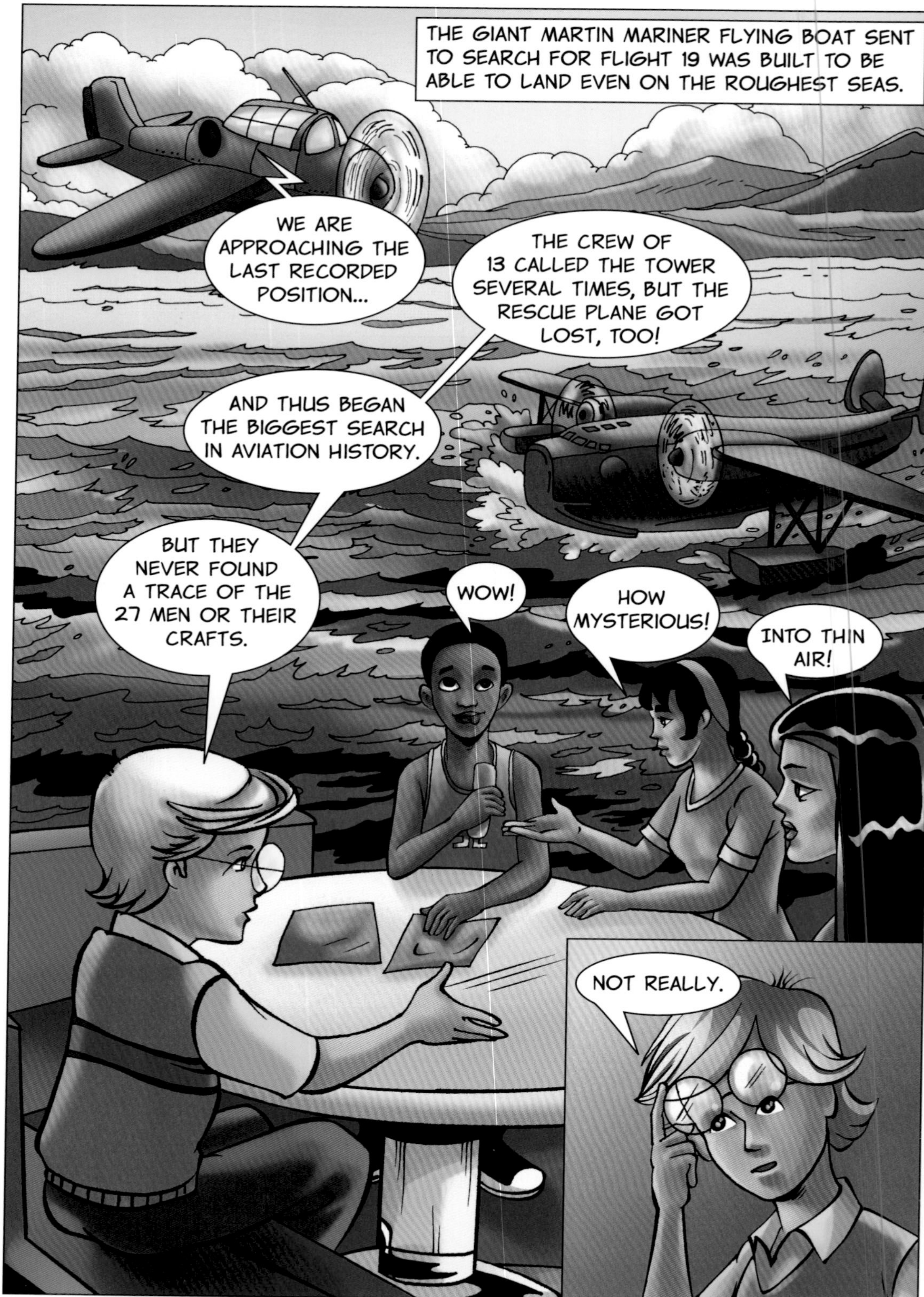
THE GIANT MARTIN MARINER FLYING BOAT SENT TO SEARCH FOR FLIGHT 19 WAS BUILT TO BE ABLE TO LAND EVEN ON THE ROUGHEST SEAS.
WE ARE APPROACHING THE LAST RECORDED POSITION...
THE CREW OF 13 CALLED THE TOWER SEVERAL TIMES, BUT THE RESCUE PLANE GOT LOST, TOO!
AND THUS BEGAN THE BIGGEST SEARCH IN AVIATION HISTORY.
BUT THEY NEVER FOUND A TRACE OF THE 27 MEN OR THEIR CRAFTS.
WOW!
HOW MYSTERIOUS!
INTO THIN AIR!
NOT REALLY.

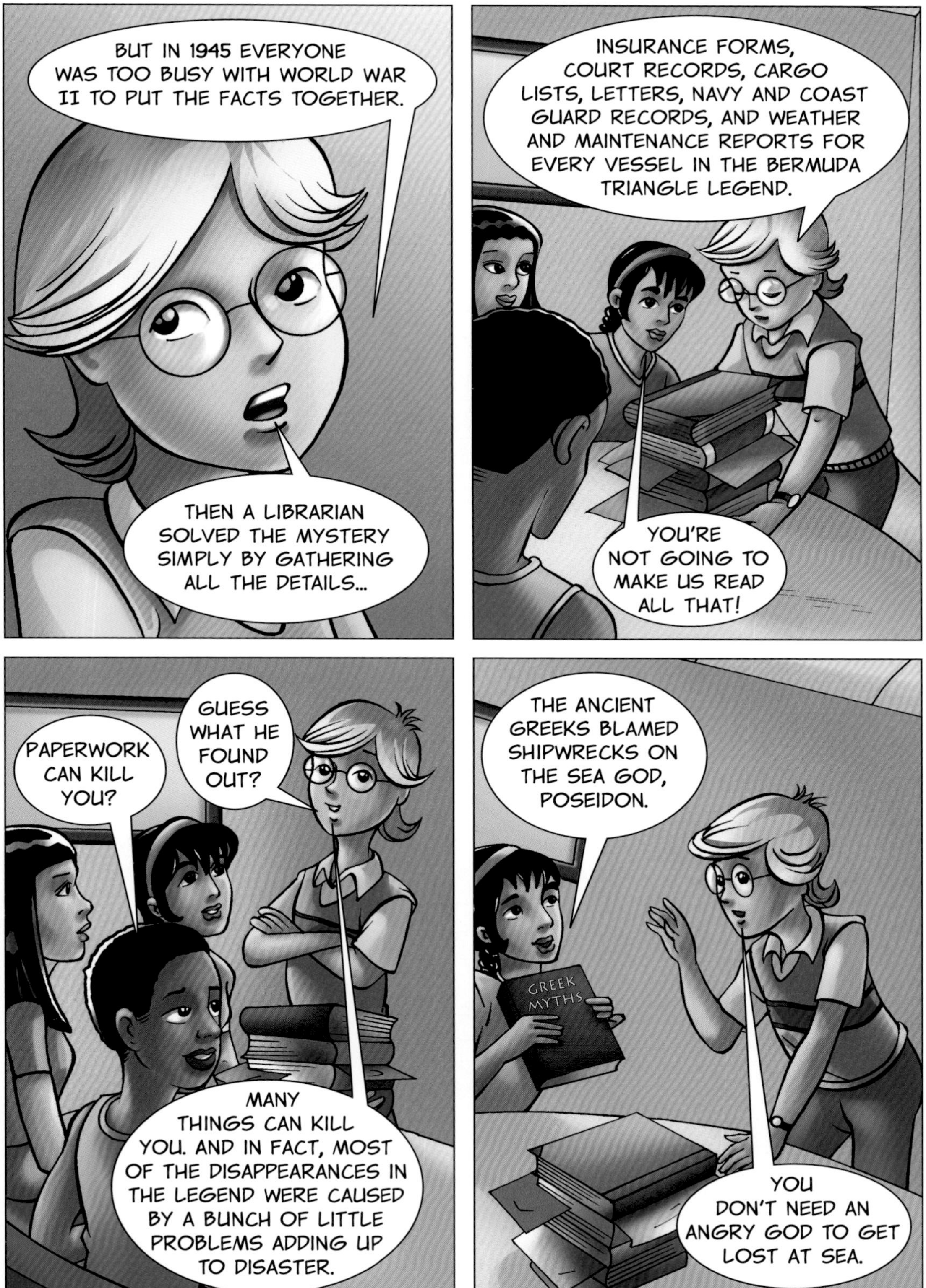
BUT IN 1945 EVERYONE WAS TOO BUSY WITH WORLD WAR II TO PUT THE FACTS TOGETHER.
THEN A LIBRARIAN SOLVED THE MYSTERY SIMPLY BY GATHERING ALL THE DETAILS...
INSURANCE FORMS, COURT RECORDS, CARGO LISTS, LETTERS, NAVY AND COAST GUARD RECORDS, AND WEATHER AND MAINTENANCE REPORTS FOR EVERY VESSEL IN THE BERMUDA TRIANGLE LEGEND.
YOU'RE NOT GOING TO MAKE US READ ALL THAT!
PAPERWORK CAN KILL YOU?
GUESS WHAT HE FOUND OUT?
MANY THINGS CAN KILL YOU. AND IN FACT, MOST OF THE DISAPPEARANCES IN THE LEGEND WERE CAUSED BY A BUNCH OF LITTLE PROBLEMS ADDING UP TO DISASTER.
THE ANCIENT GREEKS BLAMED SHIPWRECKS ON THE SEA GOD, POSEIDON.
GREEK MYTHS
YOU DON'T NEED AN ANGRY GOD TO GET LOST AT SEA.

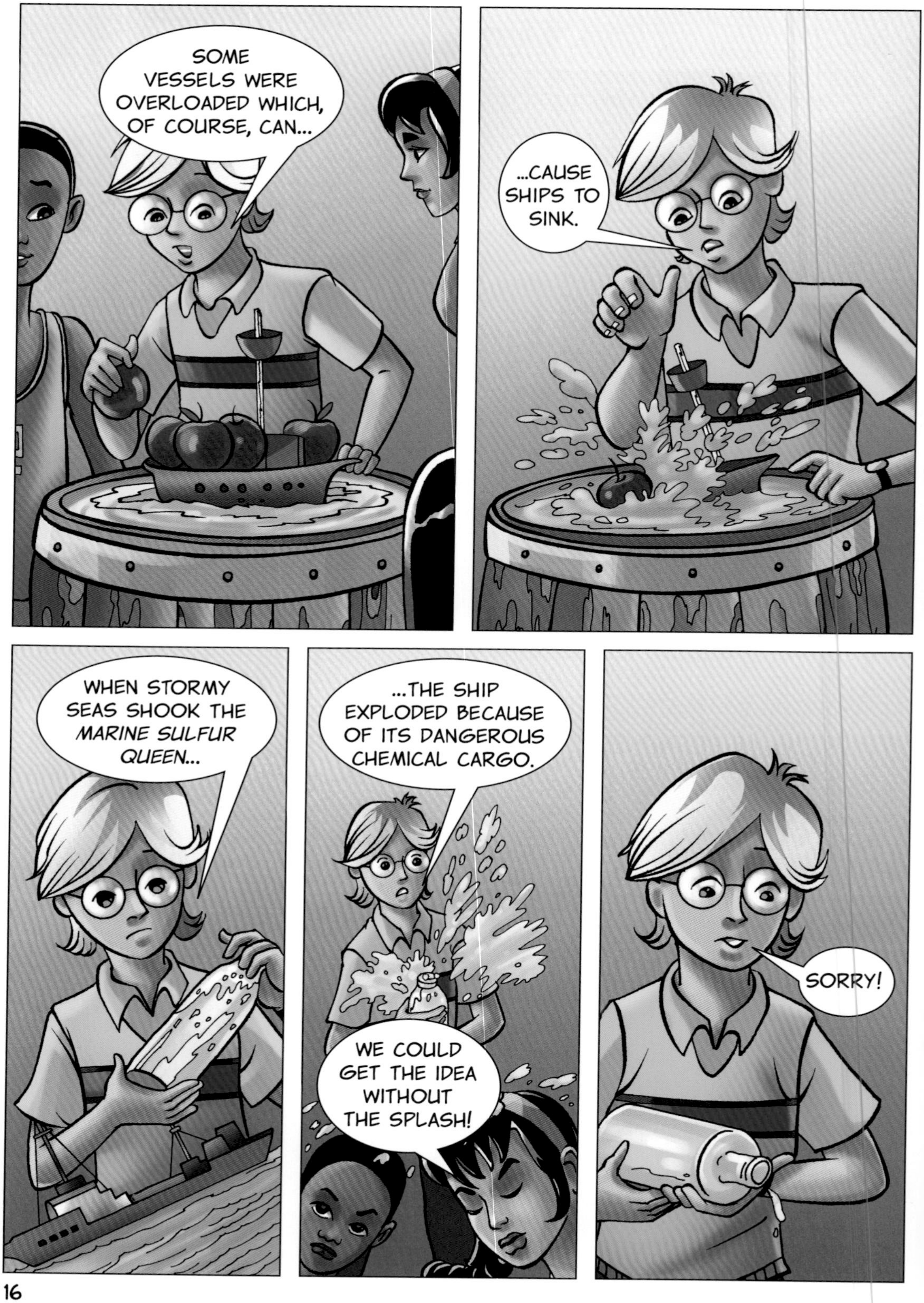
SOME VESSELS WERE OVERLOADED WHICH, OF COURSE, CAN...
...CAUSE SHIPS TO SINK.
WHEN STORMY SEAS SHOOK THE *MARINE SULFUR QUEEN*...
...THE SHIP EXPLODED BECAUSE OF ITS DANGEROUS CHEMICAL CARGO.
WE COULD GET THE IDEA WITHOUT THE SPLASH!
SORRY!

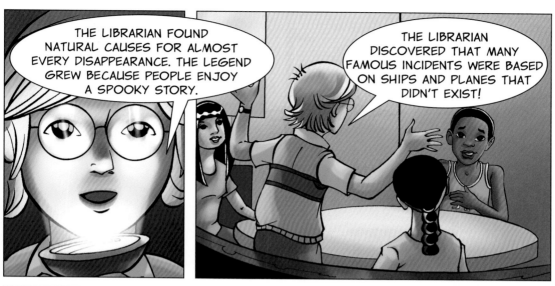

THE LIBRARIAN FOUND NATURAL CAUSES FOR ALMOST EVERY DISAPPEARANCE. THE LEGEND GREW BECAUSE PEOPLE ENJOY A SPOOKY STORY.

THE LIBRARIAN DISCOVERED THAT MANY FAMOUS INCIDENTS WERE BASED ON SHIPS AND PLANES THAT DIDN'T EXIST!

MANY VESSELS WERE LOST HUNDREDS OF MILES OUTSIDE THE TRIANGLE.

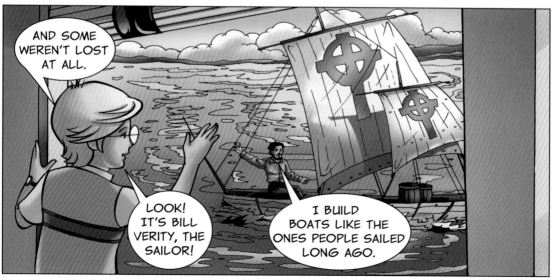

AND SOME WEREN'T LOST AT ALL.

LOOK! IT'S BILL VERITY, THE SAILOR!

I BUILD BOATS LIKE THE ONES PEOPLE SAILED LONG AGO.

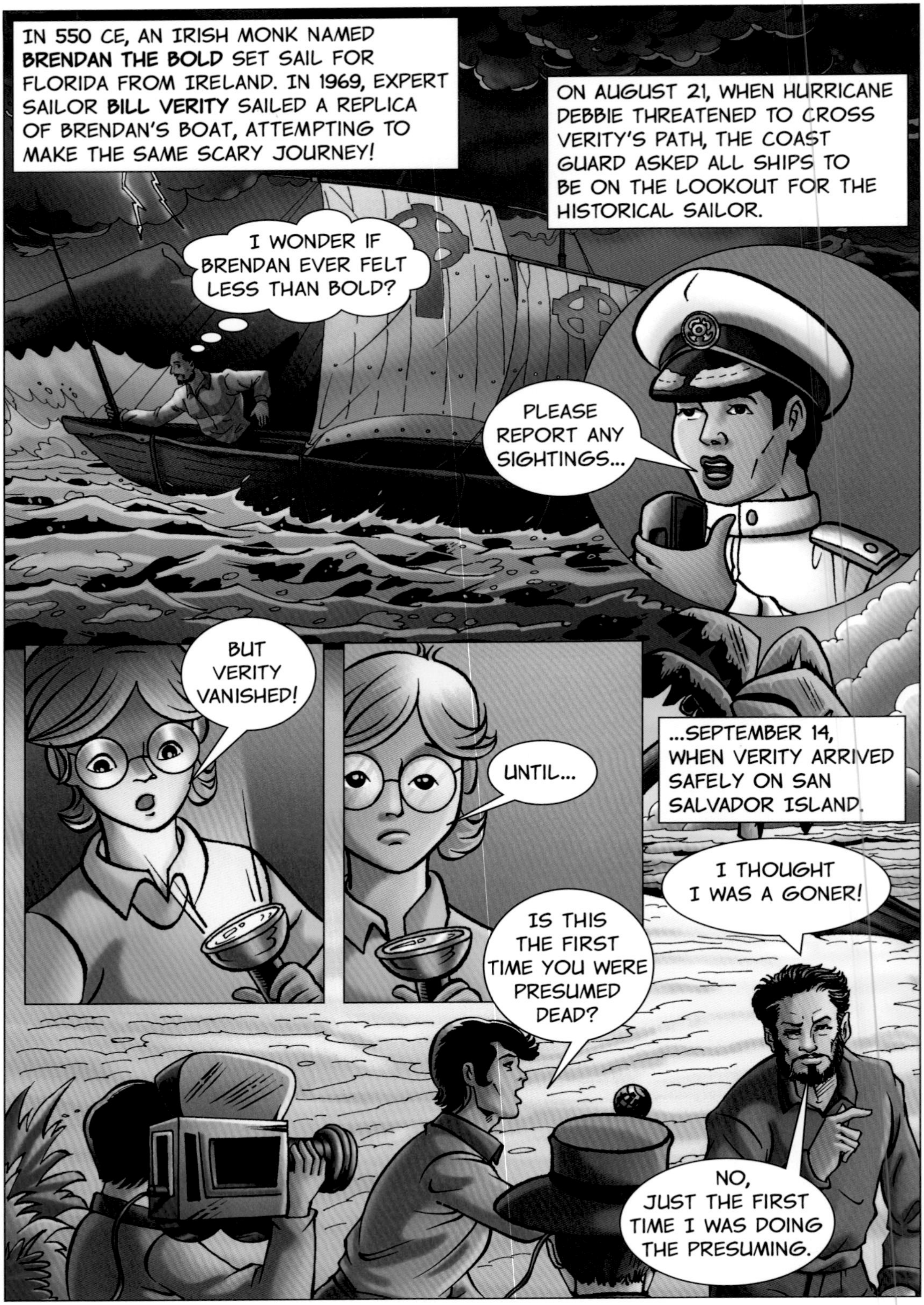
IN 550 CE, AN IRISH MONK NAMED BRENDAN THE BOLD SET SAIL FOR FLORIDA FROM IRELAND. IN 1969, EXPERT SAILOR BILL VERITY SAILED A REPLICA OF BRENDAN'S BOAT, ATTEMPTING TO MAKE THE SAME SCARY JOURNEY!
I WONDER IF BRENDAN EVER FELT LESS THAN BOLD?
ON AUGUST 21, WHEN HURRICANE DEBBIE THREATENED TO CROSS VERITY'S PATH, THE COAST GUARD ASKED ALL SHIPS TO BE ON THE LOOKOUT FOR THE HISTORICAL SAILOR.
PLEASE REPORT ANY SIGHTINGS...
BUT VERITY VANISHED!
UNTIL...
...SEPTEMBER 14, WHEN VERITY ARRIVED SAFELY ON SAN SALVADOR ISLAND.
I THOUGHT I WAS A GONER!
IS THIS THE FIRST TIME YOU WERE PRESUMED DEAD?
NO, JUST THE FIRST TIME I WAS DOING THE PRESUMING.

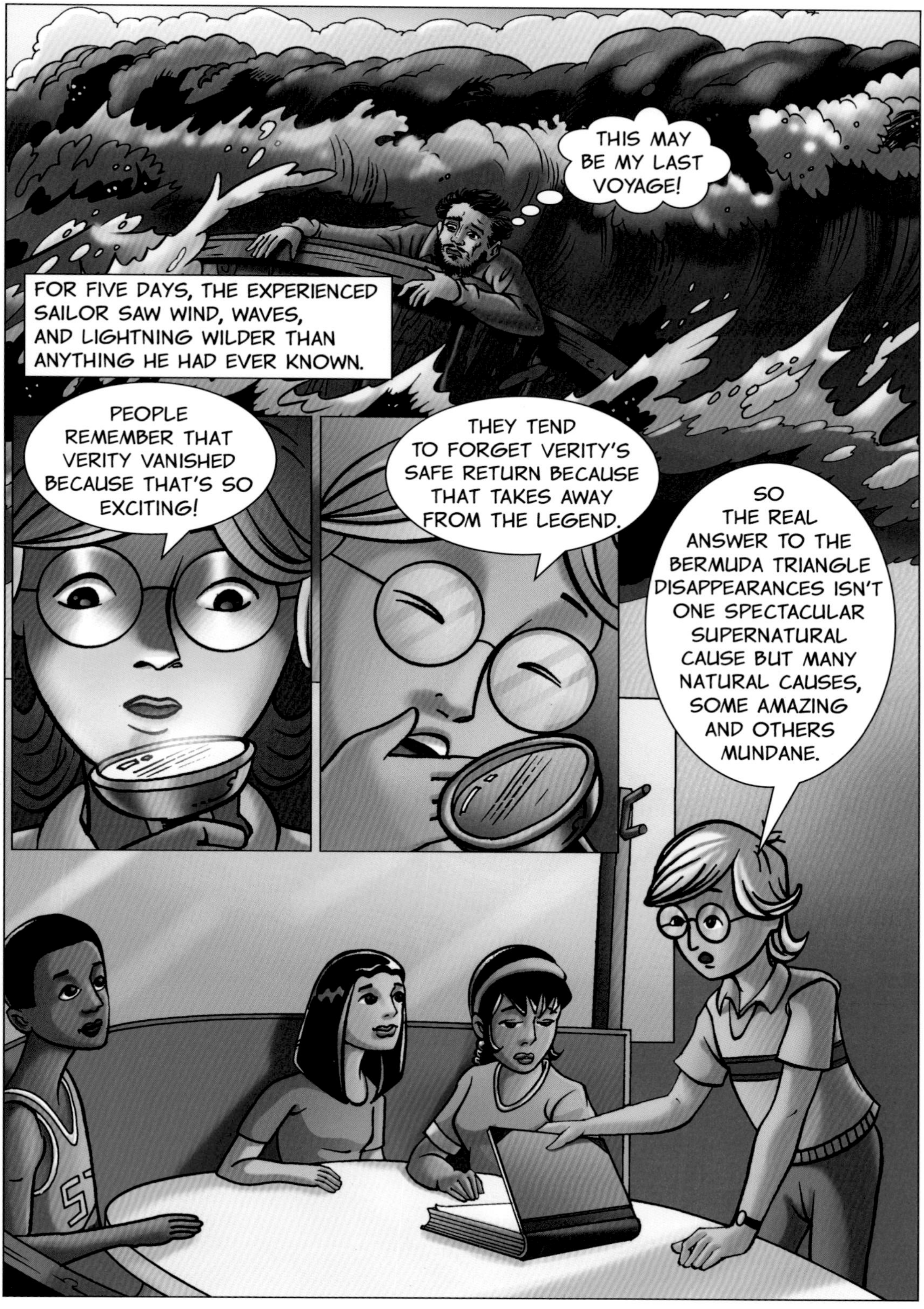
THIS MAY BE MY LAST VOYAGE!
FOR FIVE DAYS, THE EXPERIENCED SAILOR SAW WIND, WAVES, AND LIGHTNING WILDER THAN ANYTHING HE HAD EVER KNOWN.
PEOPLE REMEMBER THAT VERITY VANISHED BECAUSE THAT'S SO EXCITING!
THEY TEND TO FORGET VERITY'S SAFE RETURN BECAUSE THAT TAKES AWAY FROM THE LEGEND.
SO THE REAL ANSWER TO THE BERMUDA TRIANGLE DISAPPEARANCES ISN'T ONE SPECTACULAR SUPERNATURAL CAUSE BUT MANY NATURAL CAUSES, SOME AMAZING AND OTHERS MUNDANE.

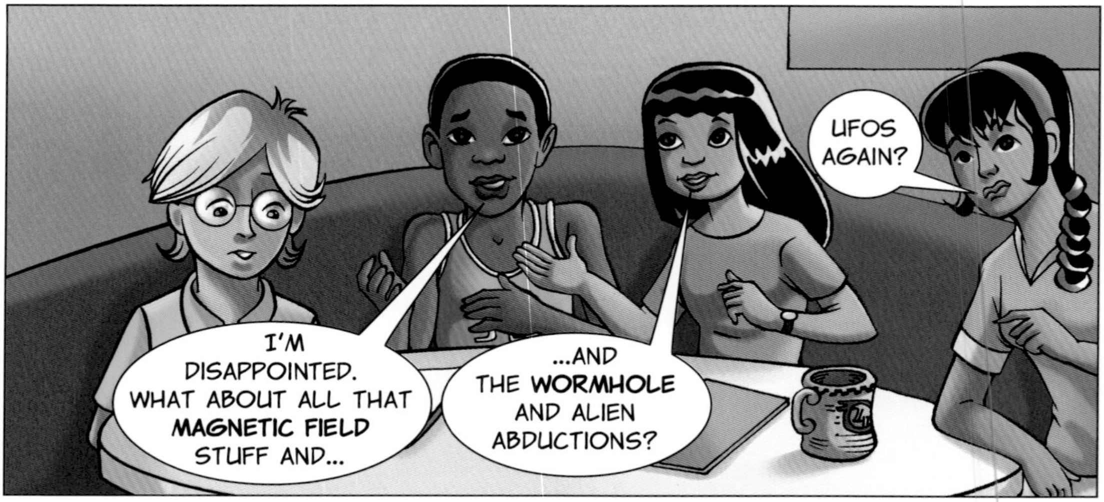
UFOS AGAIN?
I'M DISAPPOINTED. WHAT ABOUT ALL THAT **MAGNETIC FIELD** STUFF AND...
...AND THE **WORMHOLE** AND ALIEN ABDUCTIONS?

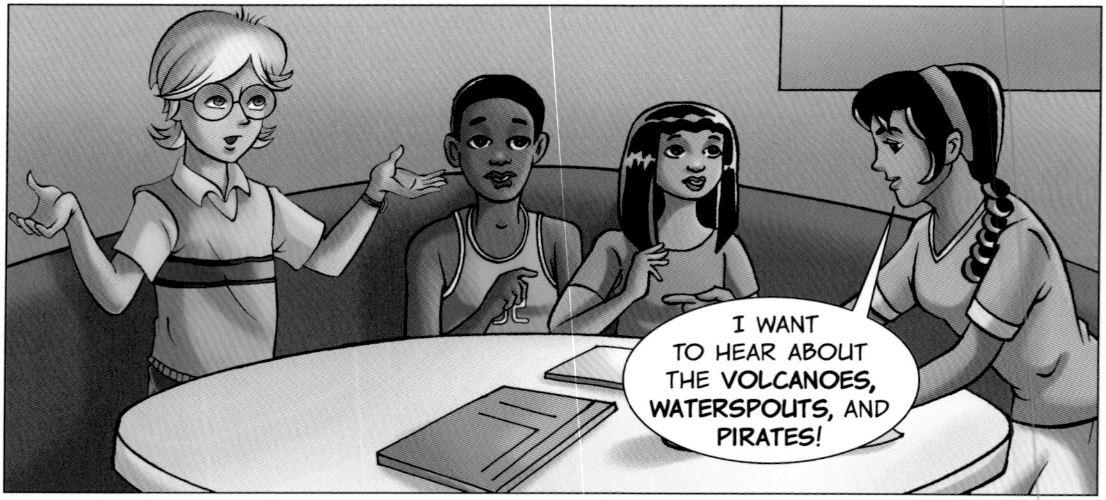
I WANT TO HEAR ABOUT THE **VOLCANOES, WATERSPOUTS,** AND **PIRATES!**

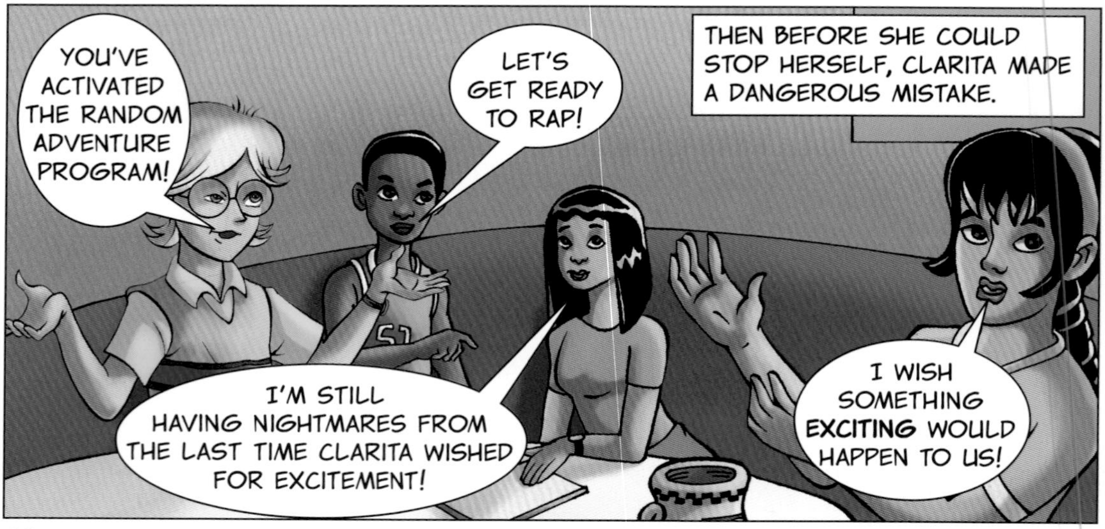
THEN BEFORE SHE COULD STOP HERSELF, CLARITA MADE A DANGEROUS MISTAKE.
YOU'VE ACTIVATED THE RANDOM ADVENTURE PROGRAM!
LET'S GET READY TO RAP!
I'M STILL HAVING NIGHTMARES FROM THE LAST TIME CLARITA WISHED FOR EXCITEMENT!
I WISH SOMETHING **EXCITING** WOULD HAPPEN TO US!

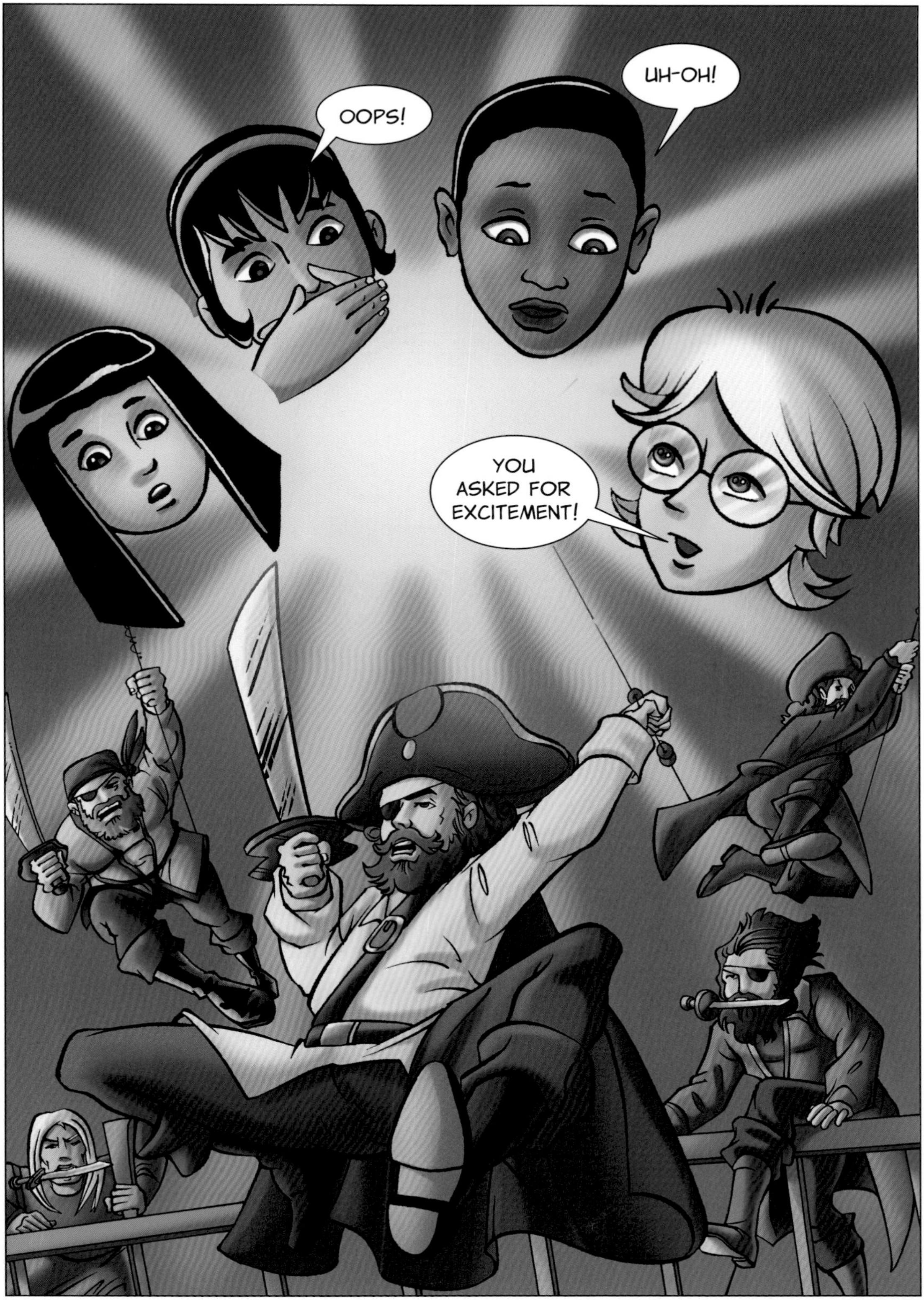
OOPS!
UH-OH!
YOU ASKED FOR EXCITEMENT!

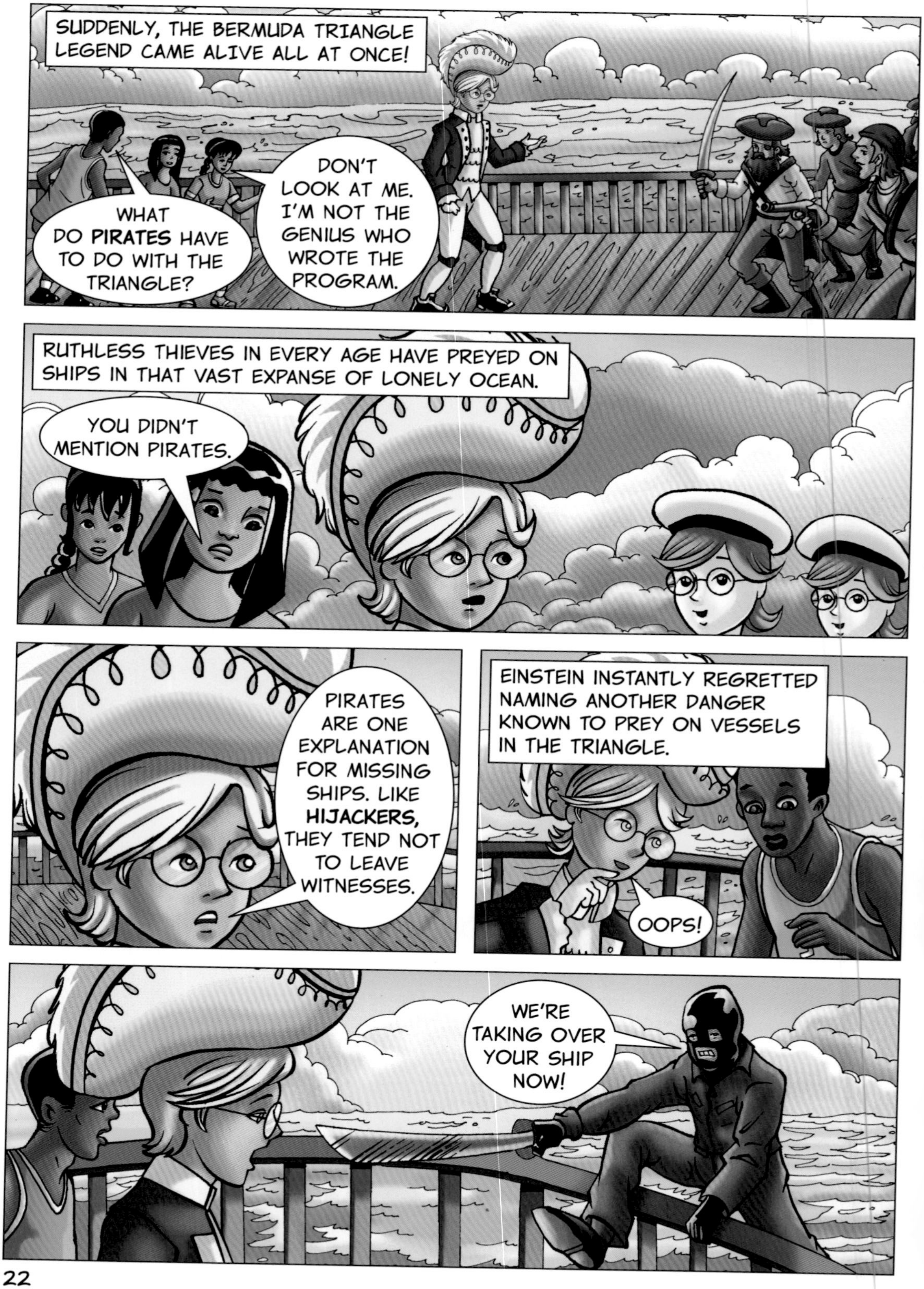
SUDDENLY, THE BERMUDA TRIANGLE LEGEND CAME ALIVE ALL AT ONCE!
WHAT DO PIRATES HAVE TO DO WITH THE TRIANGLE?
DON'T LOOK AT ME. I'M NOT THE GENIUS WHO WROTE THE PROGRAM.
RUTHLESS THIEVES IN EVERY AGE HAVE PREYED ON SHIPS IN THAT VAST EXPANSE OF LONELY OCEAN.
YOU DIDN'T MENTION PIRATES.
PIRATES ARE ONE EXPLANATION FOR MISSING SHIPS. LIKE HIJACKERS, THEY TEND NOT TO LEAVE WITNESSES.
EINSTEIN INSTANTLY REGRETTED NAMING ANOTHER DANGER KNOWN TO PREY ON VESSELS IN THE TRIANGLE.
OOPS!
WE'RE TAKING OVER YOUR SHIP NOW!

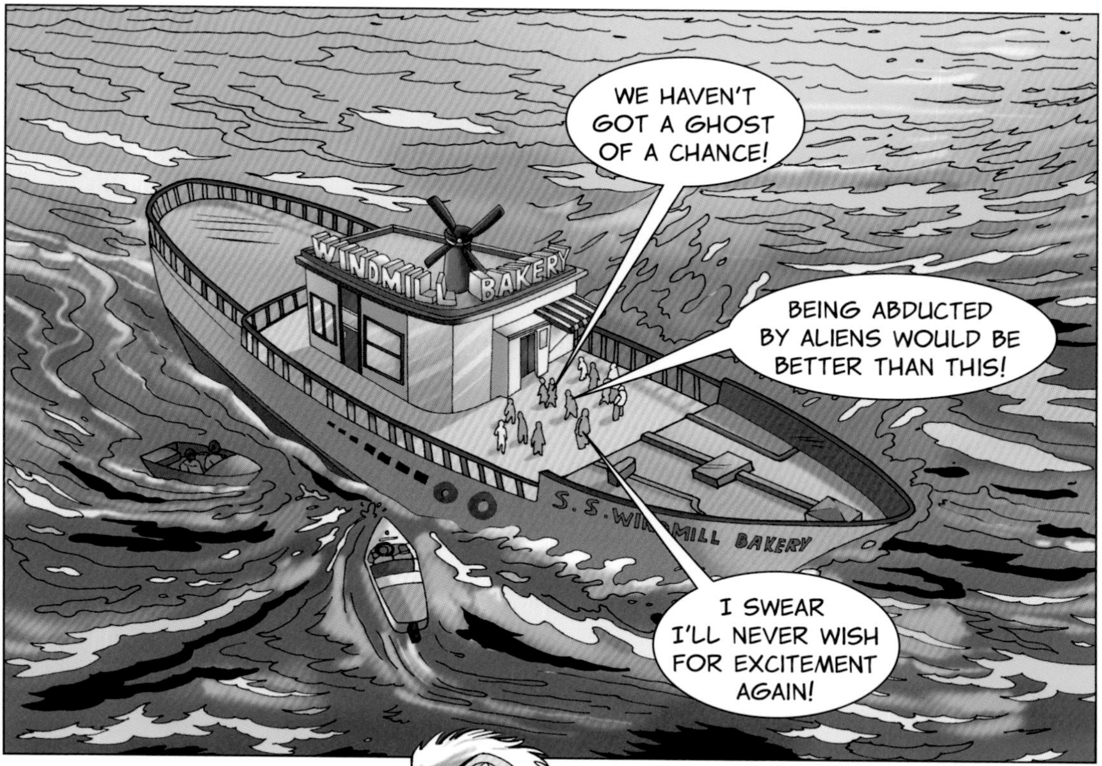
WE HAVEN'T GOT A GHOST OF A CHANCE!
WINDMILL BAKERY
BEING ABDUCTED BY ALIENS WOULD BE BETTER THAN THIS!
S.S. WINDMILL BAKERY
I SWEAR I'LL NEVER WISH FOR EXCITEMENT AGAIN!

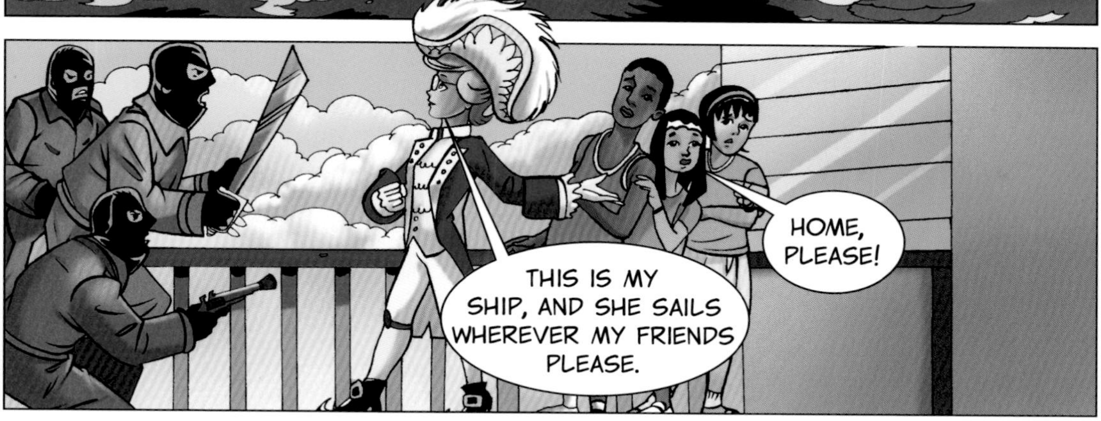
HOME, PLEASE!
THIS IS MY SHIP, AND SHE SAILS WHEREVER MY FRIENDS PLEASE.

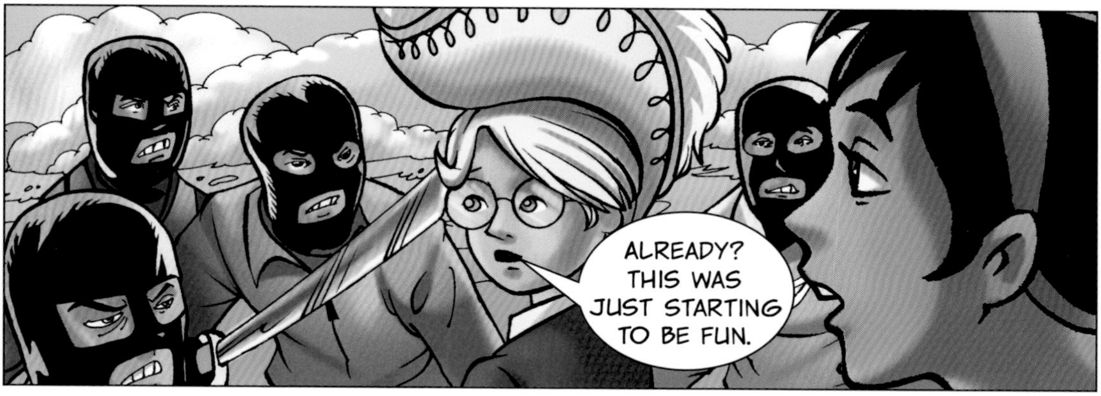
ALREADY? THIS WAS JUST STARTING TO BE FUN.

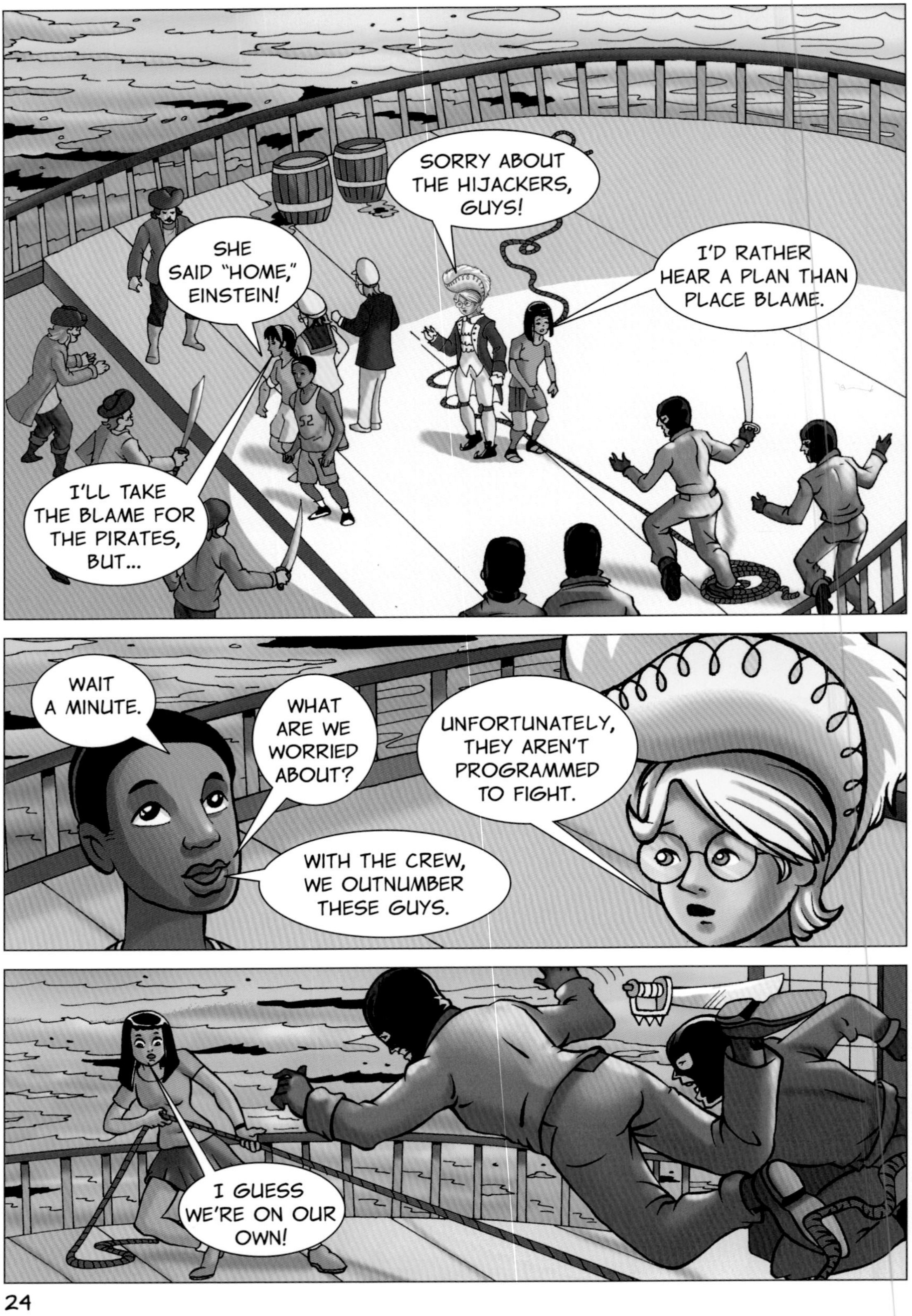
SHE SAID "HOME," EINSTEIN!
I'LL TAKE THE BLAME FOR THE PIRATES, BUT...
SORRY ABOUT THE HIJACKERS, GUYS!
I'D RATHER HEAR A PLAN THAN PLACE BLAME.
WAIT A MINUTE.
WHAT ARE WE WORRIED ABOUT?
WITH THE CREW, WE OUTNUMBER THESE GUYS.
UNFORTUNATELY, THEY AREN'T PROGRAMMED TO FIGHT.
I GUESS WE'RE ON OUR OWN!

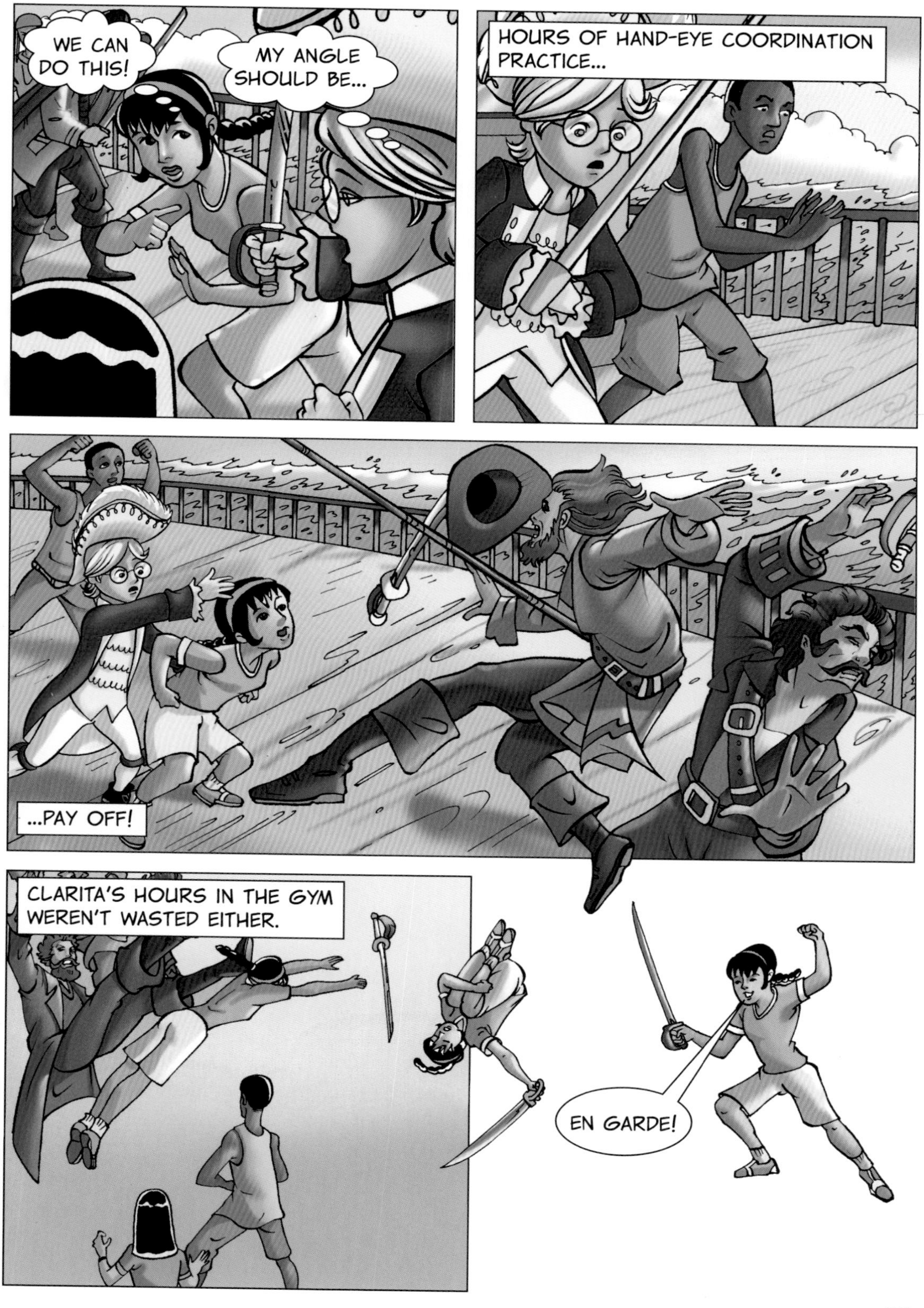
WE CAN DO THIS!
MY ANGLE SHOULD BE...
HOURS OF HAND-EYE COORDINATION PRACTICE...
...PAY OFF!
CLARITA'S HOURS IN THE GYM WEREN'T WASTED EITHER.
EN GARDE!

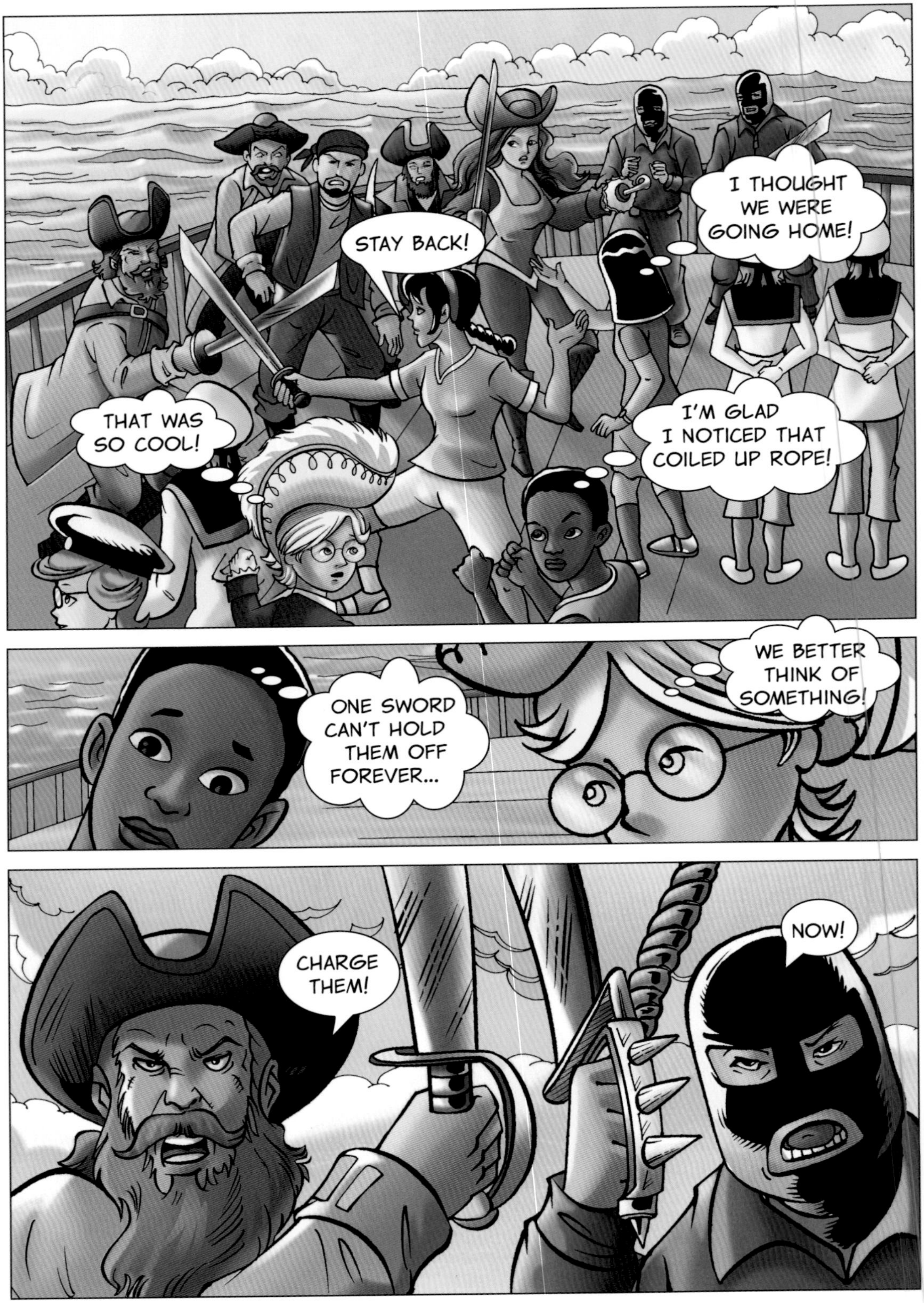
STAY BACK!
I THOUGHT WE WERE GOING HOME!
THAT WAS SO COOL!
I'M GLAD I NOTICED THAT COILED UP ROPE!
ONE SWORD CAN'T HOLD THEM OFF FOREVER...
WE BETTER THINK OF SOMETHING!
CHARGE THEM!
NOW!

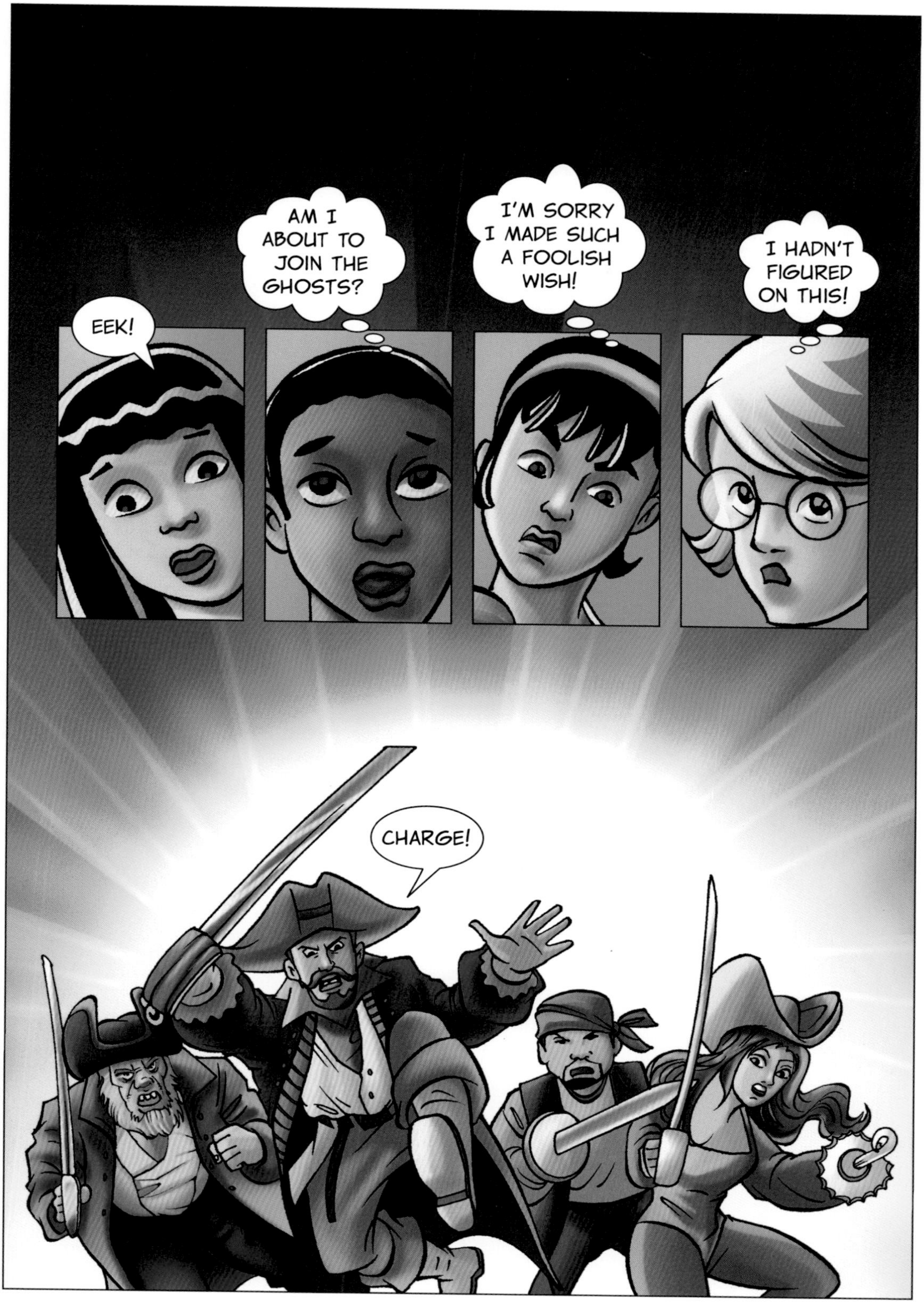
EEK!
AM I ABOUT TO JOIN THE GHOSTS?
I'M SORRY I MADE SUCH A FOOLISH WISH!
I HADN'T FIGURED ON THIS!
CHARGE!

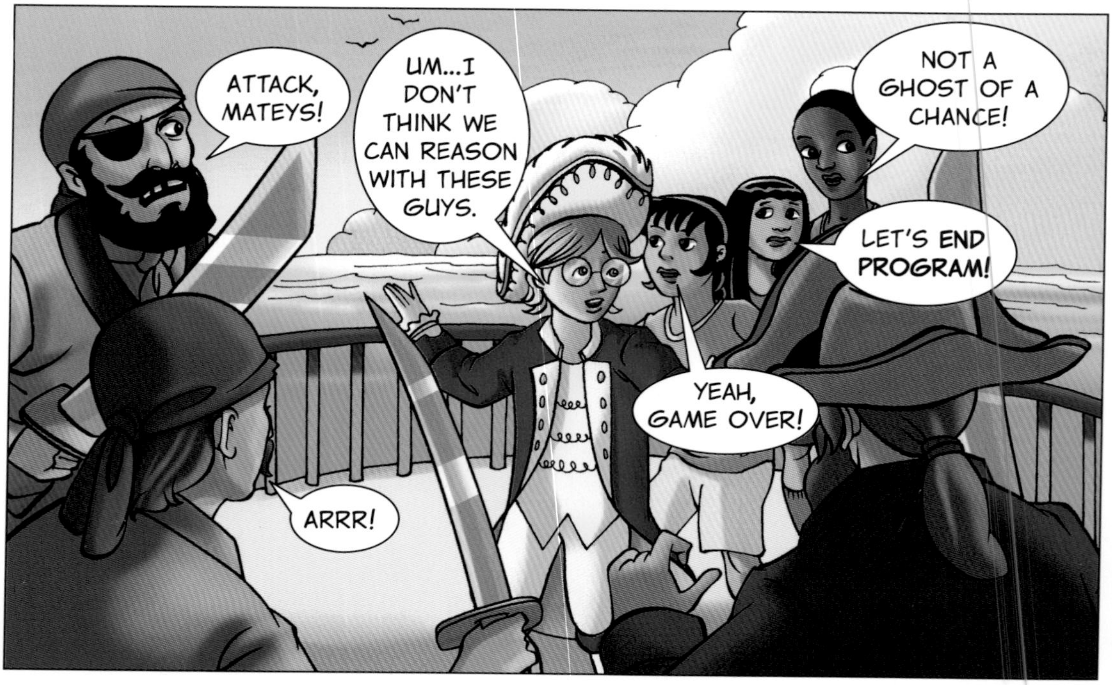
ATTACK, MATEYS!
UM...I DON'T THINK WE CAN REASON WITH THESE GUYS.
NOT A GHOST OF A CHANCE!
LET'S END PROGRAM!
YEAH, GAME OVER!
ARRR!

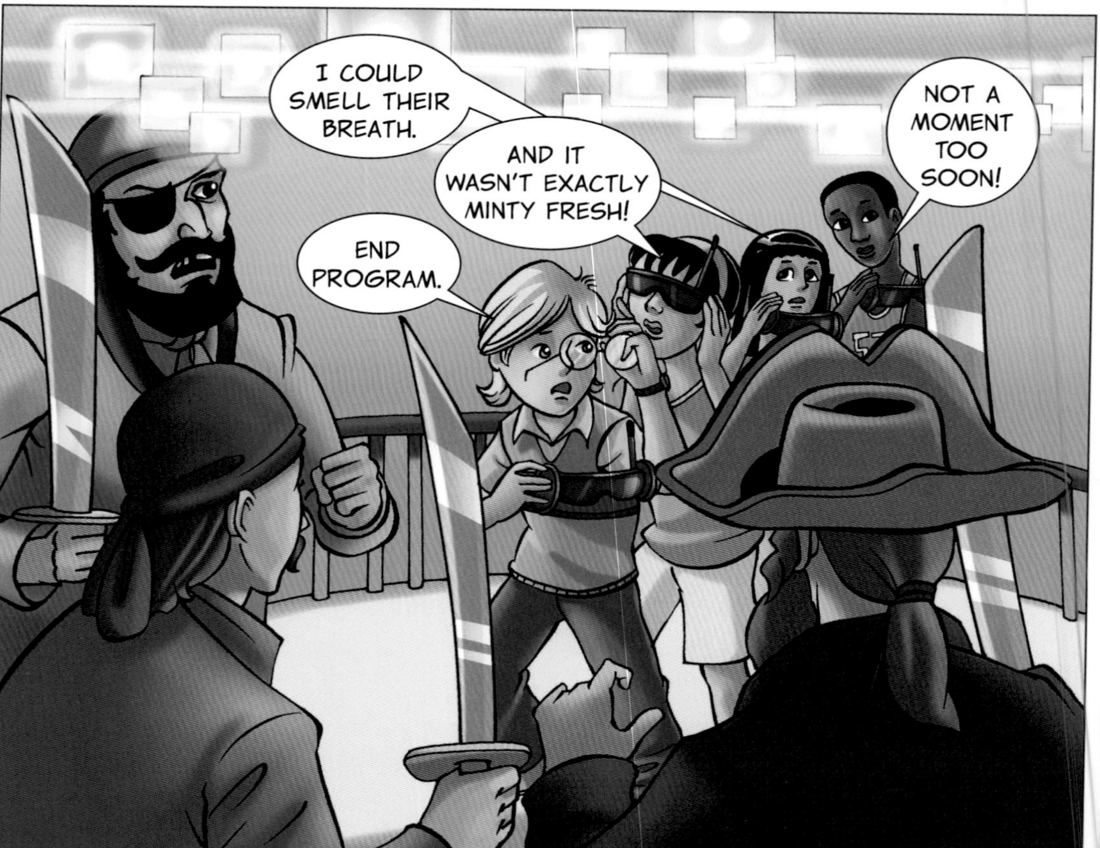
I COULD SMELL THEIR BREATH.
AND IT WASN'T EXACTLY MINTY FRESH!
NOT A MOMENT TOO SOON!
END PROGRAM.

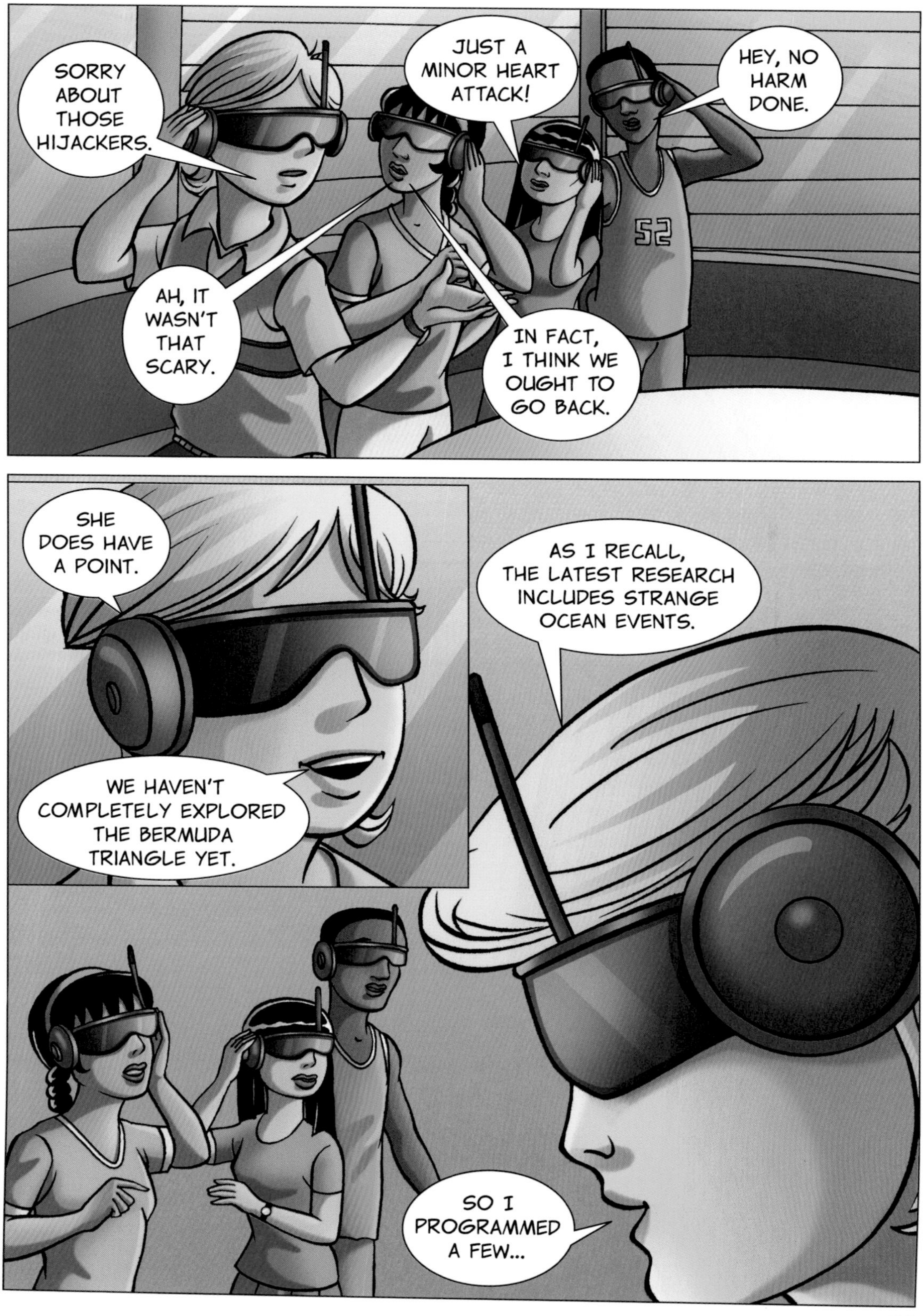
SORRY ABOUT THOSE HIJACKERS.
AH, IT WASN'T THAT SCARY.
JUST A MINOR HEART ATTACK!
IN FACT, I THINK WE OUGHT TO GO BACK.
HEY, NO HARM DONE.
SHE DOES HAVE A POINT.
WE HAVEN'T COMPLETELY EXPLORED THE BERMUDA TRIANGLE YET.
AS I RECALL, THE LATEST RESEARCH INCLUDES STRANGE OCEAN EVENTS.
SO I PROGRAMMED A FEW...

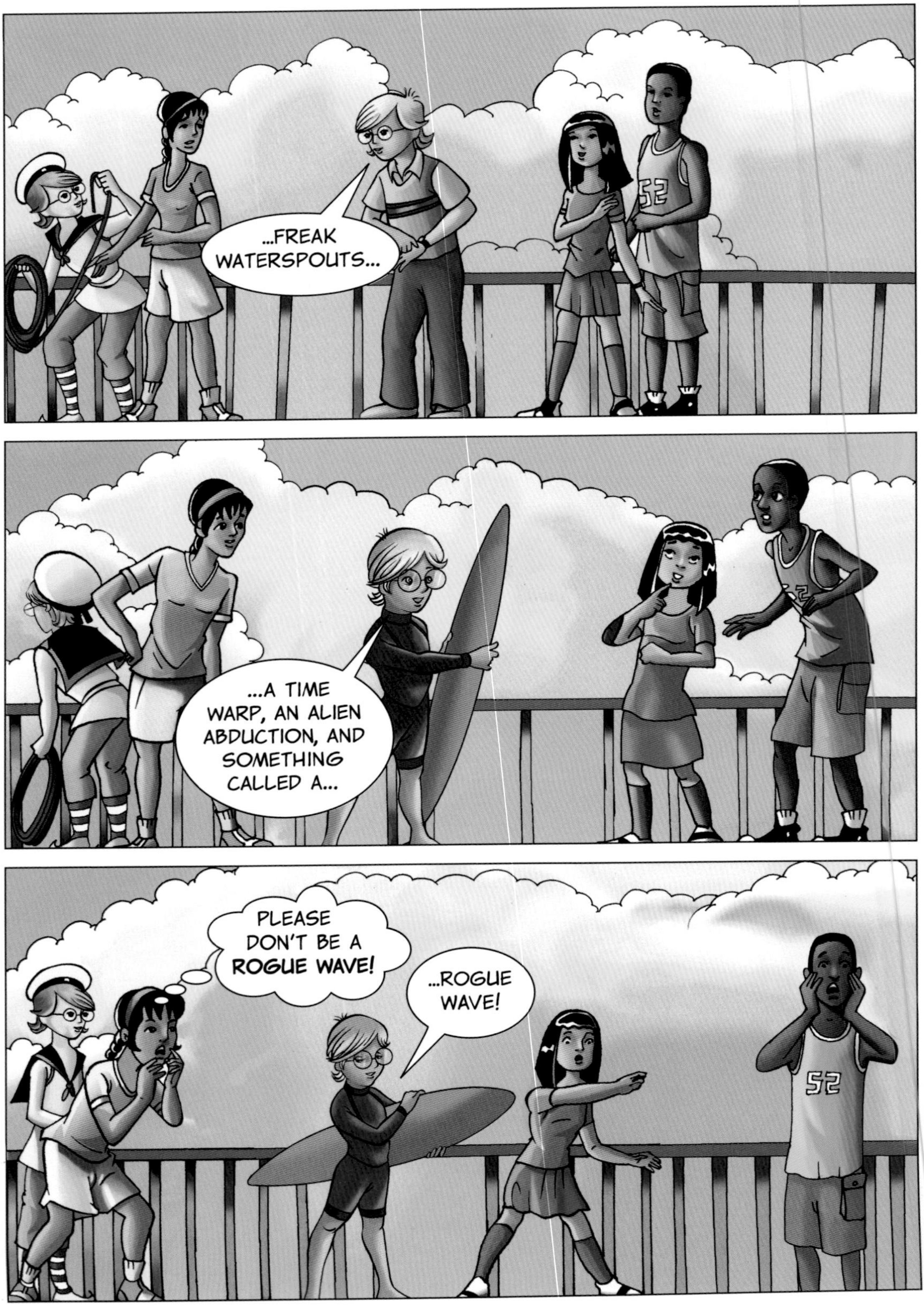
...FREAK WATERSPOUTS...
...A TIME WARP, AN ALIEN ABDUCTION, AND SOMETHING CALLED A...
PLEASE DON'T BE A **ROGUE WAVE!**
...ROGUE WAVE!

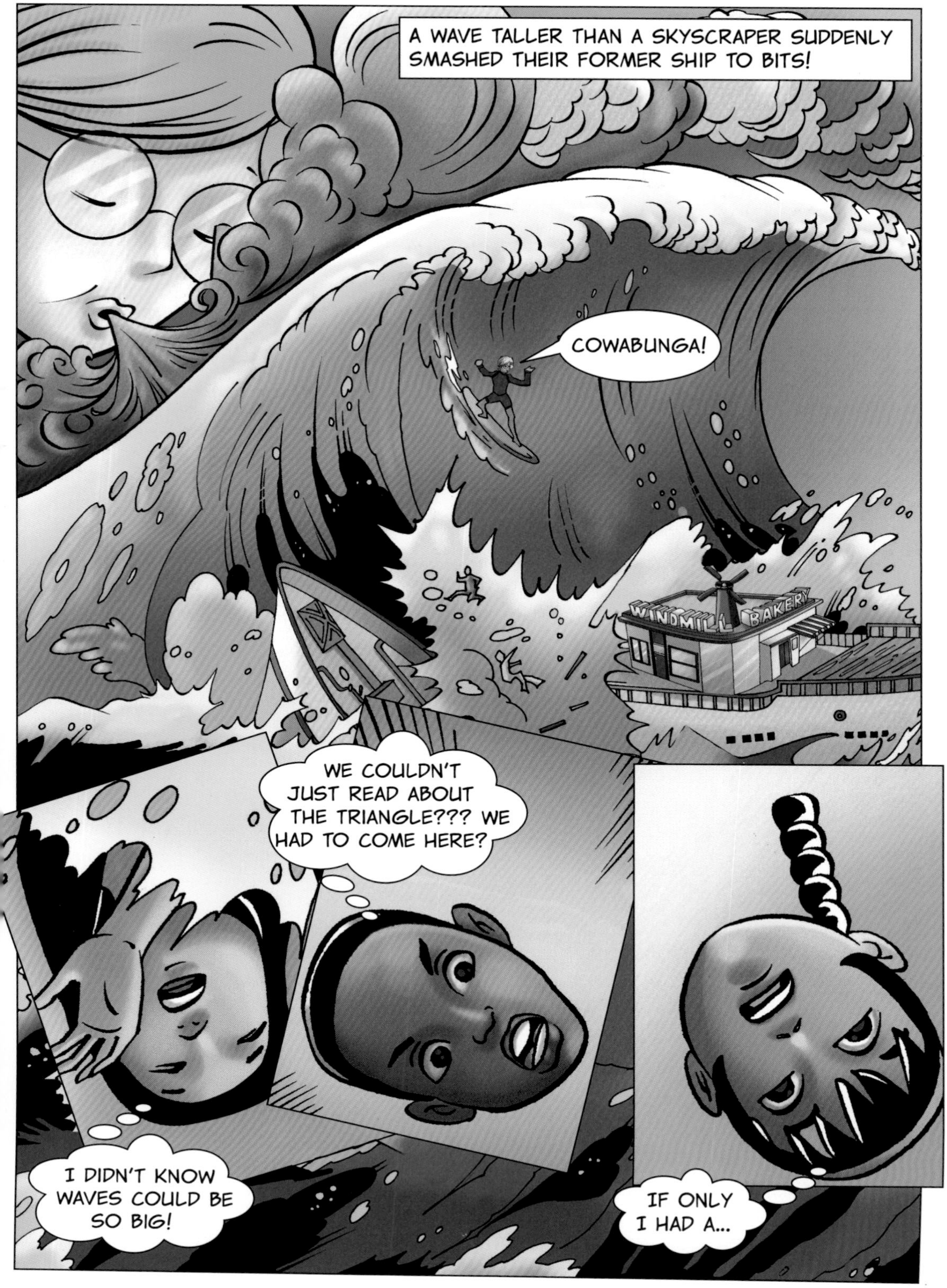
A WAVE TALLER THAN A SKYSCRAPER SUDDENLY SMASHED THEIR FORMER SHIP TO BITS!
COWABUNGA!
WINDMILL BAKERY
WE COULDN'T JUST READ ABOUT THE TRIANGLE??? WE HAD TO COME HERE?
I DIDN'T KNOW WAVES COULD BE SO BIG!
IF ONLY I HAD A...

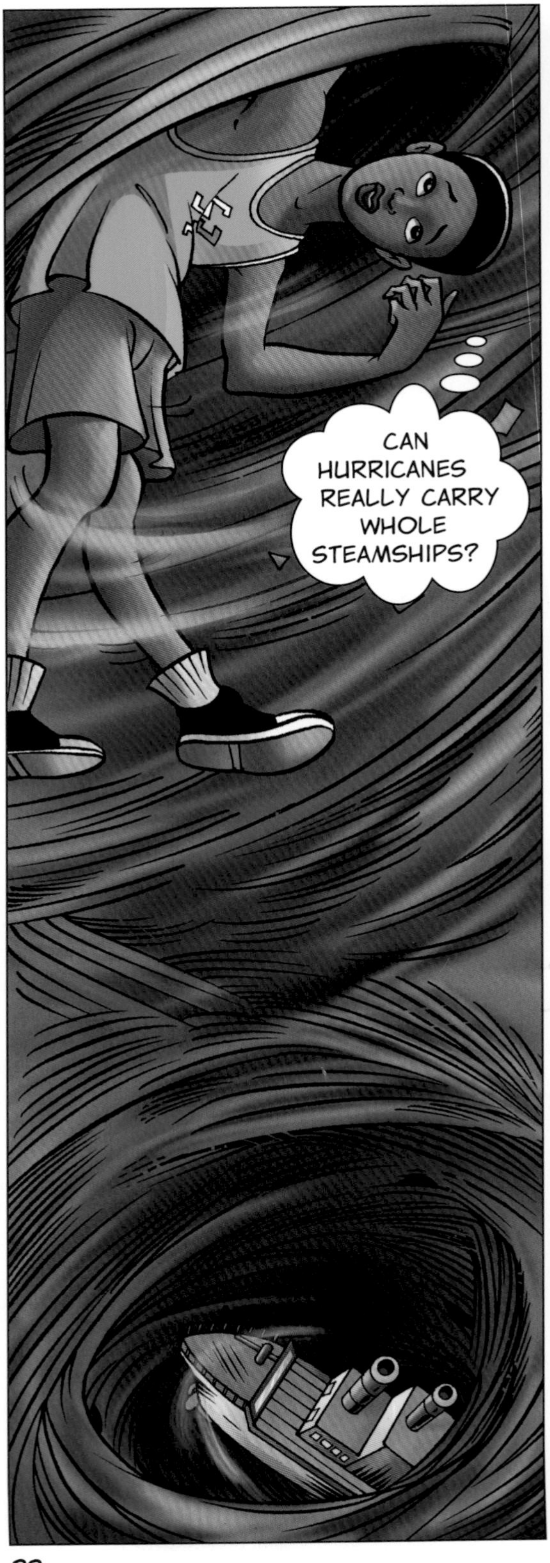
CAN HURRICANES REALLY CARRY WHOLE STEAMSHIPS?

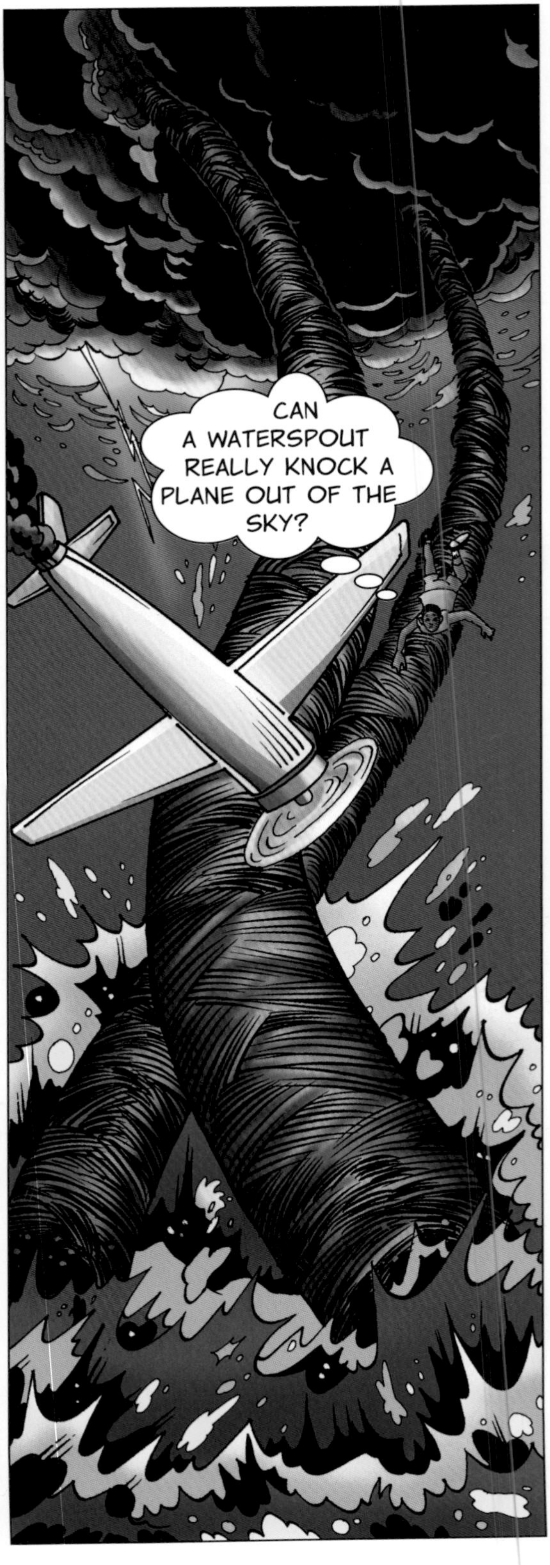
CAN A WATERSPOUT REALLY KNOCK A PLANE OUT OF THE SKY?

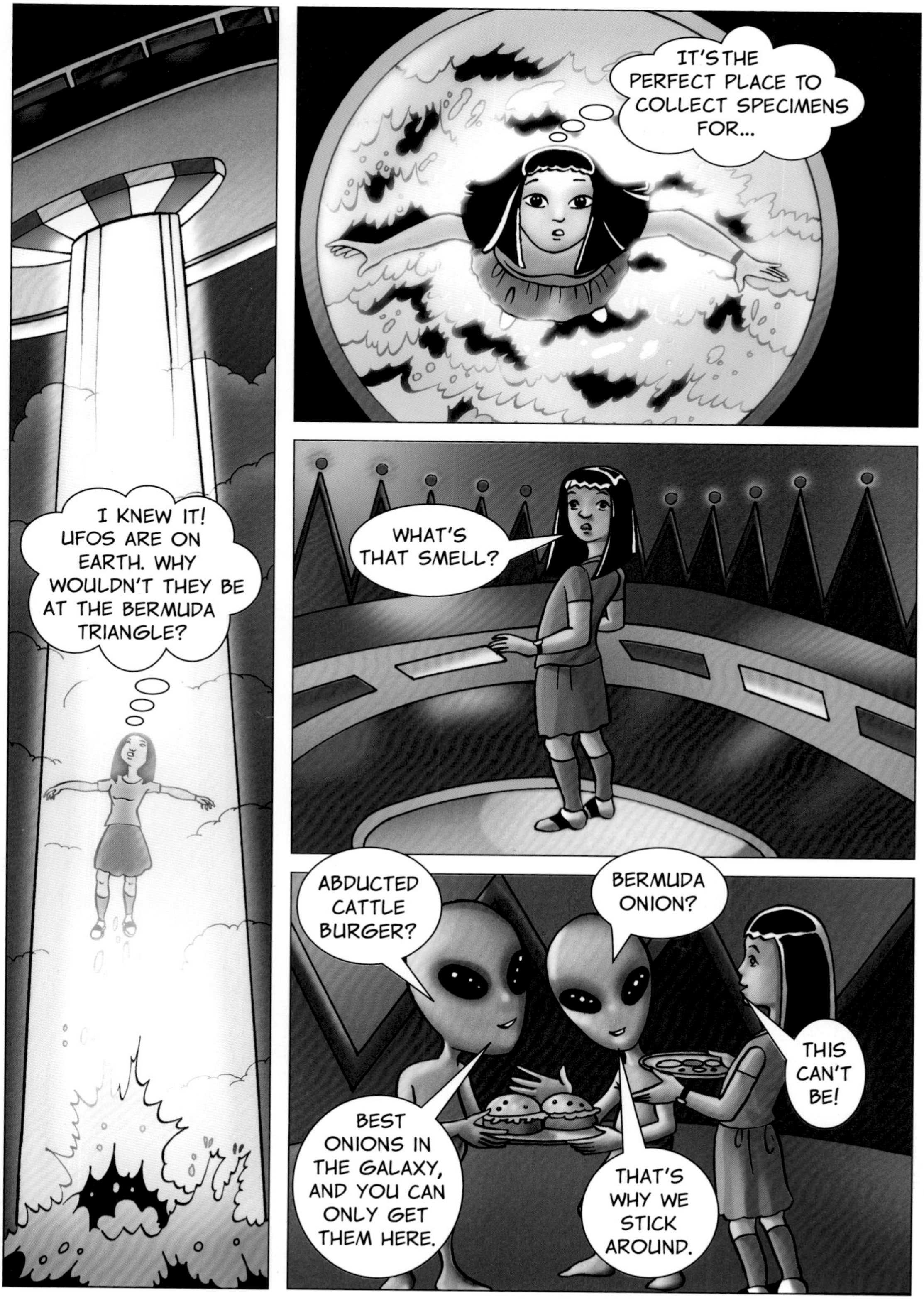
I KNEW IT! UFOS ARE ON EARTH. WHY WOULDN'T THEY BE AT THE BERMUDA TRIANGLE?
IT'S THE PERFECT PLACE TO COLLECT SPECIMENS FOR...
WHAT'S THAT SMELL?
ABDUCTED CATTLE BURGER?
BERMUDA ONION?
BEST ONIONS IN THE GALAXY, AND YOU CAN ONLY GET THEM HERE.
THAT'S WHY WE STICK AROUND.
THIS CAN'T BE!

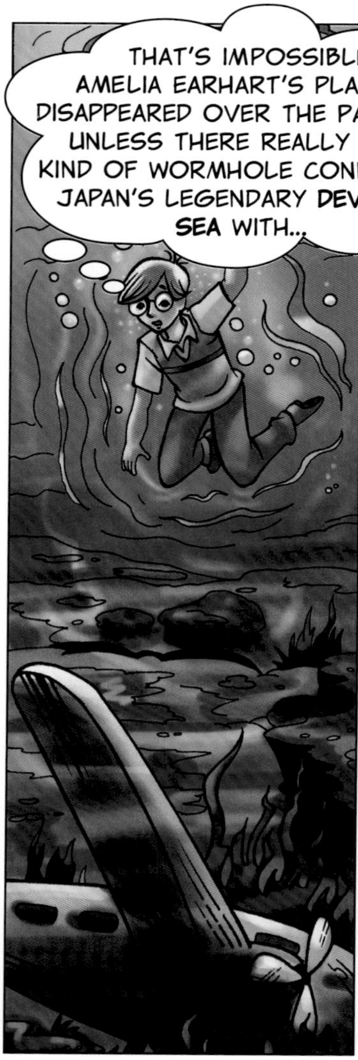
THAT'S IMPOSSIBLE! AMELIA EARHART'S PLANE DISAPPEARED OVER THE PACIFIC. UNLESS THERE REALLY IS SOME KIND OF WORMHOLE CONNECTING JAPAN'S LEGENDARY **DEVIL'S SEA** WITH...

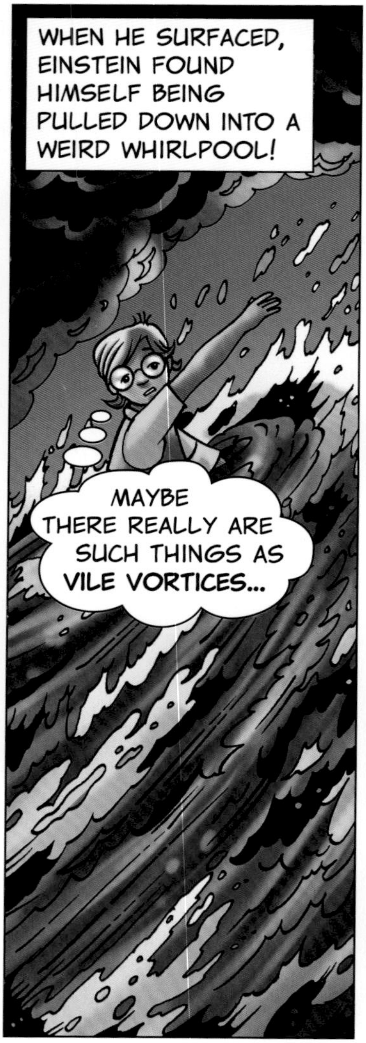
WHEN HE SURFACED, EINSTEIN FOUND HIMSELF BEING PULLED DOWN INTO A WEIRD WHIRLPOOL!
MAYBE THERE REALLY ARE SUCH THINGS AS **VILE VORTICES...**

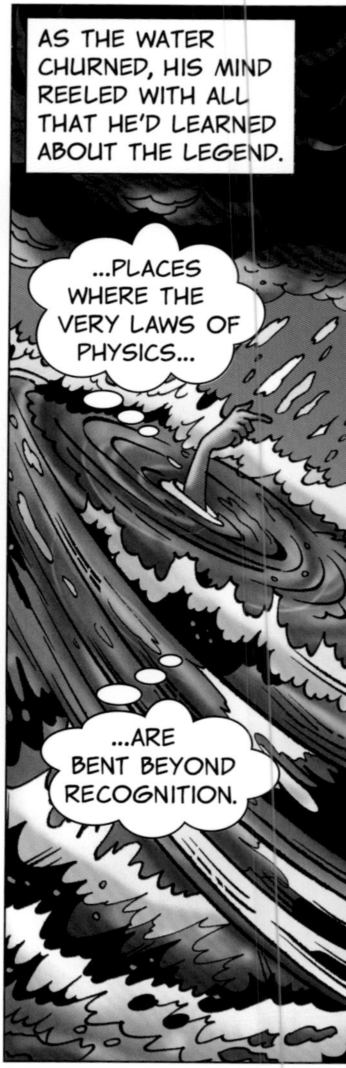
AS THE WATER CHURNED, HIS MIND REELED WITH ALL THAT HE'D LEARNED ABOUT THE LEGEND.
...PLACES WHERE THE VERY LAWS OF PHYSICS...
...ARE BENT BEYOND RECOGNITION.

WHEN THE WHIRLPOOL SUDDENLY RELEASED HIM, EINSTEIN SAW A BOAT.

TOO FAR OFF THE COAST OF FLORIDA, KID.

I'M AL SNIDER, WHO ARE YOU?

WHERE AM I?

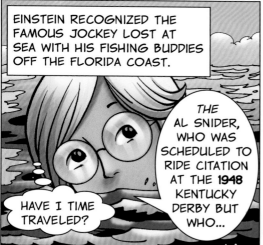

EINSTEIN RECOGNIZED THE FAMOUS JOCKEY LOST AT SEA WITH HIS FISHING BUDDIES OFF THE FLORIDA COAST.

THE AL SNIDER, WHO WAS SCHEDULED TO RIDE CITATION AT THE 1948 KENTUCKY DERBY BUT WHO...

HAVE I TIME TRAVELED?

DON'T REMIND ME, KID!

I WOULD'VE WON, IF WE HADN'T GONE FISHING IN THE...

COULD EVERYONE LOST IN THE TRIANGLE SOMEHOW STILL BE HERE?

OH, NO! I'M STARTING TO SOUND LIKE FRANK!

WE'VE GOT THE BERMUDA TRIANGLE BLUES, DOWN TO OUR SOGGY SHOES...

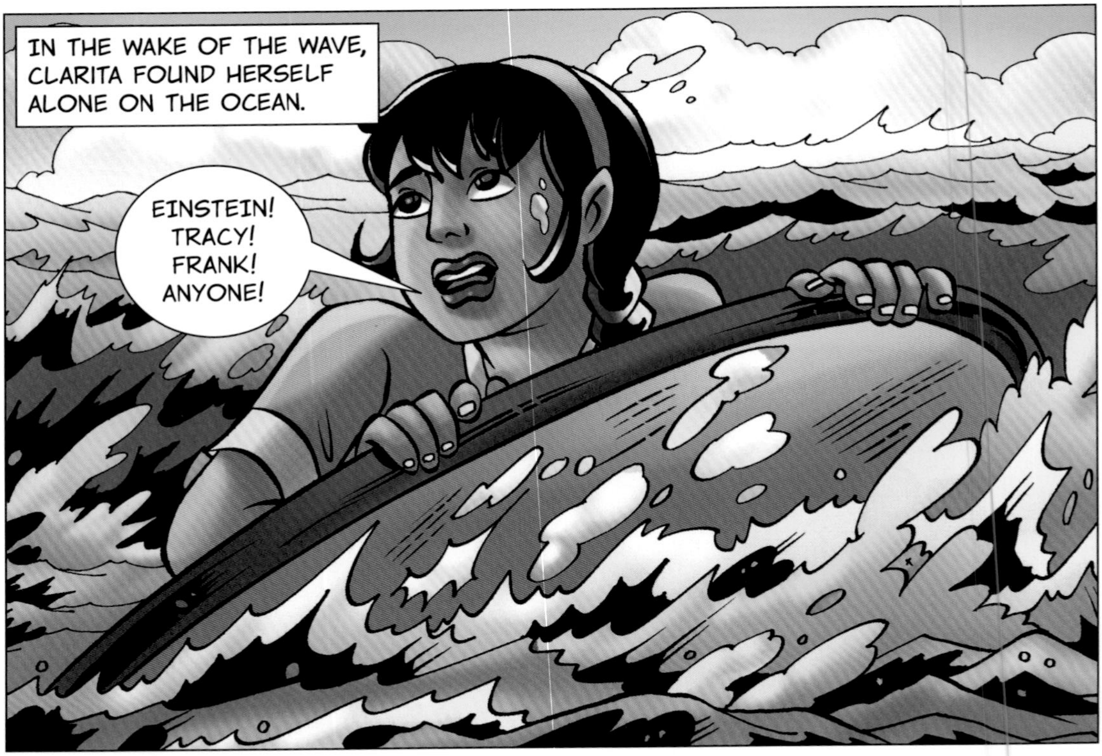
IN THE WAKE OF THE WAVE, CLARITA FOUND HERSELF ALONE ON THE OCEAN.
EINSTEIN! TRACY! FRANK! ANYONE!

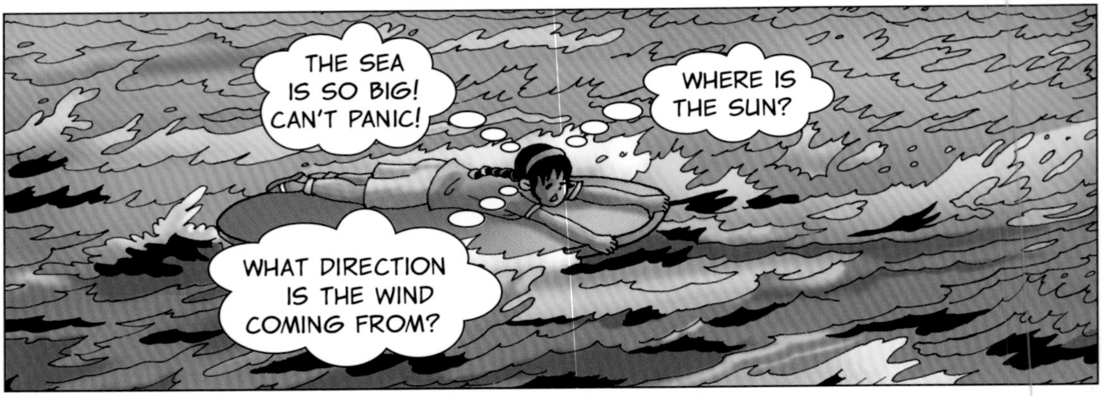
THE SEA IS SO BIG! CAN'T PANIC!
WHERE IS THE SUN?
WHAT DIRECTION IS THE WIND COMING FROM?

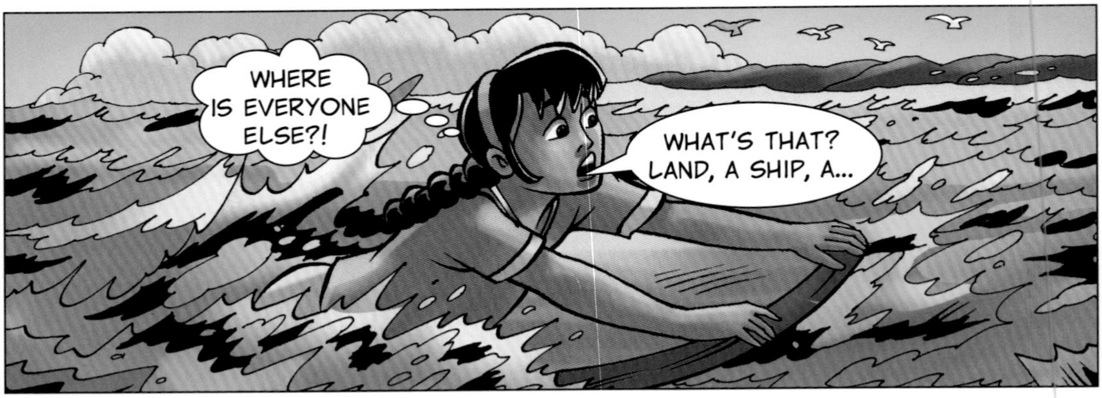
WHERE IS EVERYONE ELSE?!
WHAT'S THAT? LAND, A SHIP, A...

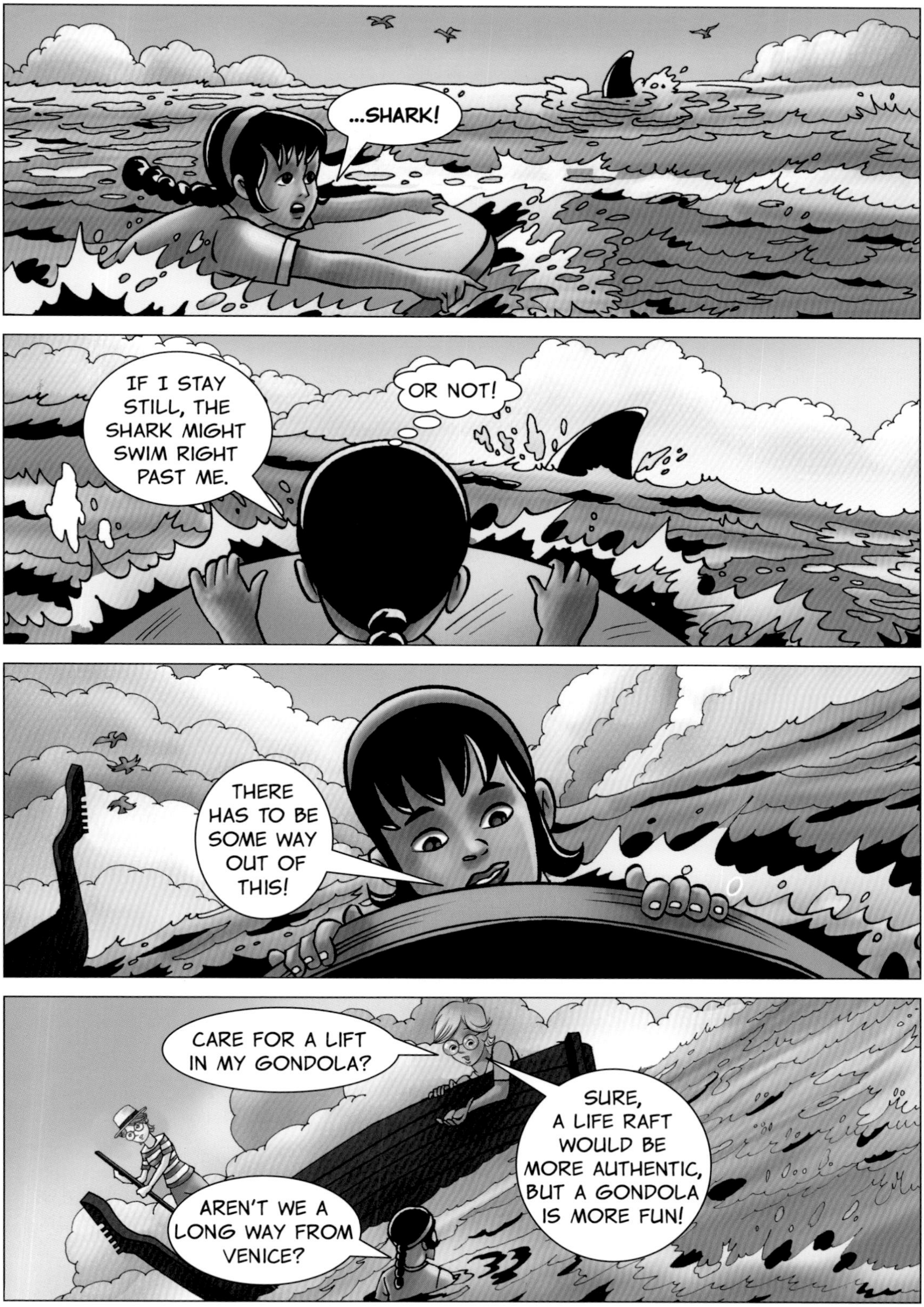
...SHARK!
IF I STAY STILL, THE SHARK MIGHT SWIM RIGHT PAST ME.
OR NOT!
THERE HAS TO BE SOME WAY OUT OF THIS!
CARE FOR A LIFT IN MY GONDOLA?
ARE'NT WE A LONG WAY FROM VENICE?
SURE, A LIFE RAFT WOULD BE MORE AUTHENTIC, BUT A GONDOLA IS MORE FUN!

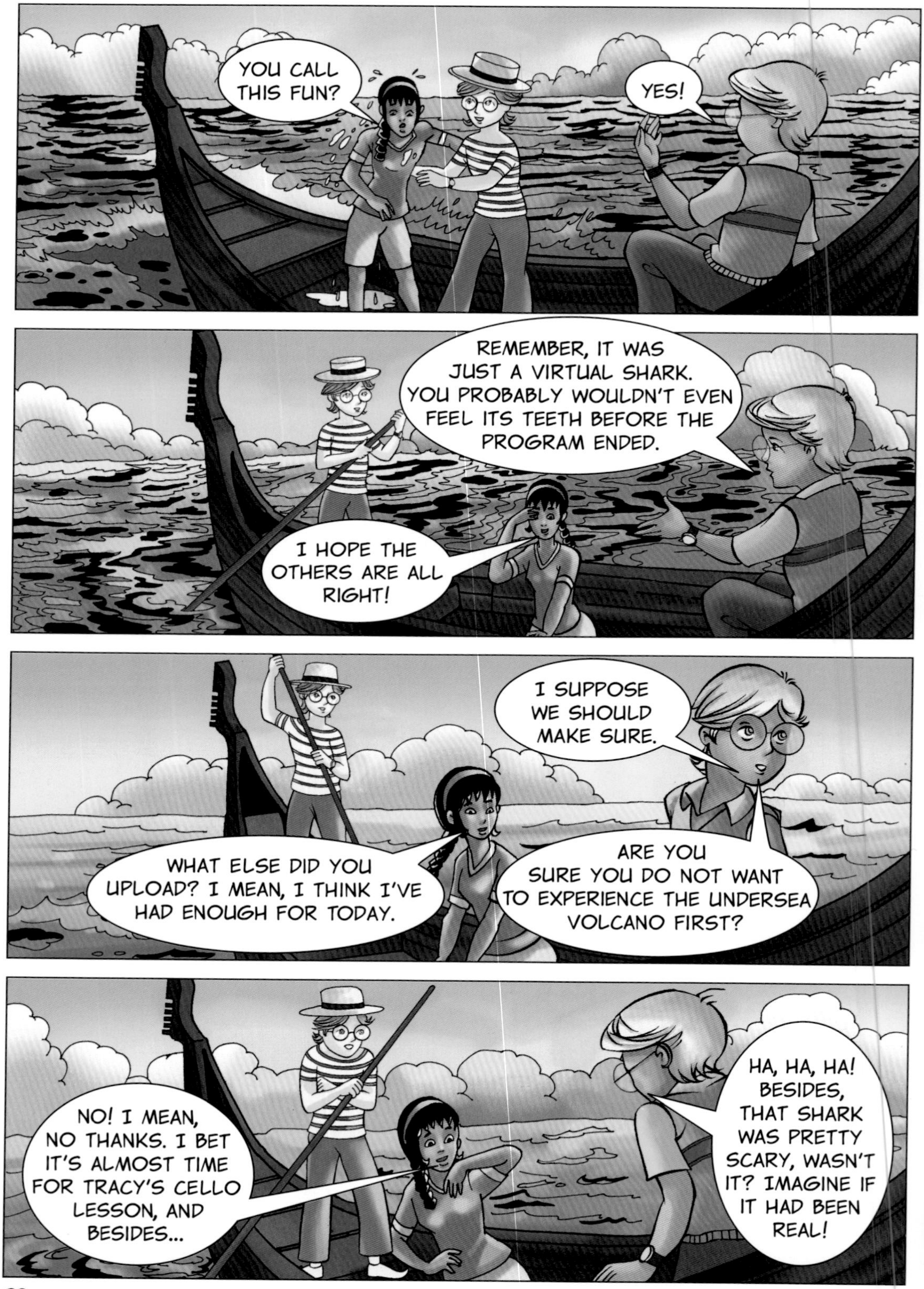
YOU CALL THIS FUN?
YES!
REMEMBER, IT WAS JUST A VIRTUAL SHARK. YOU PROBABLY WOULDN'T EVEN FEEL ITS TEETH BEFORE THE PROGRAM ENDED.
I HOPE THE OTHERS ARE ALL RIGHT!
I SUPPOSE WE SHOULD MAKE SURE.
WHAT ELSE DID YOU UPLOAD? I MEAN, I THINK I'VE HAD ENOUGH FOR TODAY.
ARE YOU SURE YOU DO NOT WANT TO EXPERIENCE THE UNDERSEA VOLCANO FIRST?
NO! I MEAN, NO THANKS. I BET IT'S ALMOST TIME FOR TRACY'S CELLO LESSON, AND BESIDES...
HA, HA, HA! BESIDES, THAT SHARK WAS PRETTY SCARY, WASN'T IT? IMAGINE IF IT HAD BEEN REAL!

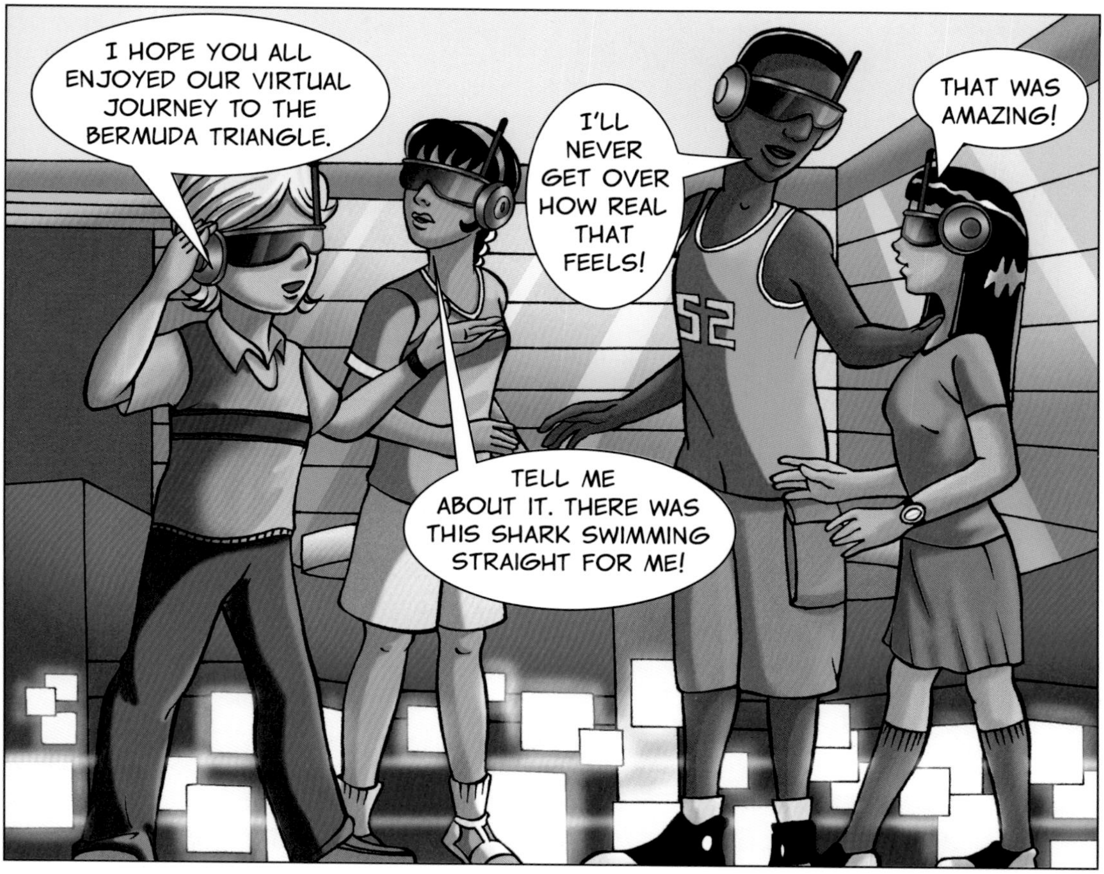
I HOPE YOU ALL ENJOYED OUR VIRTUAL JOURNEY TO THE BERMUDA TRIANGLE.
I'LL NEVER GET OVER HOW REAL THAT FEELS!
THAT WAS AMAZING!
TELL ME ABOUT IT. THERE WAS THIS SHARK SWIMMING STRAIGHT FOR ME!

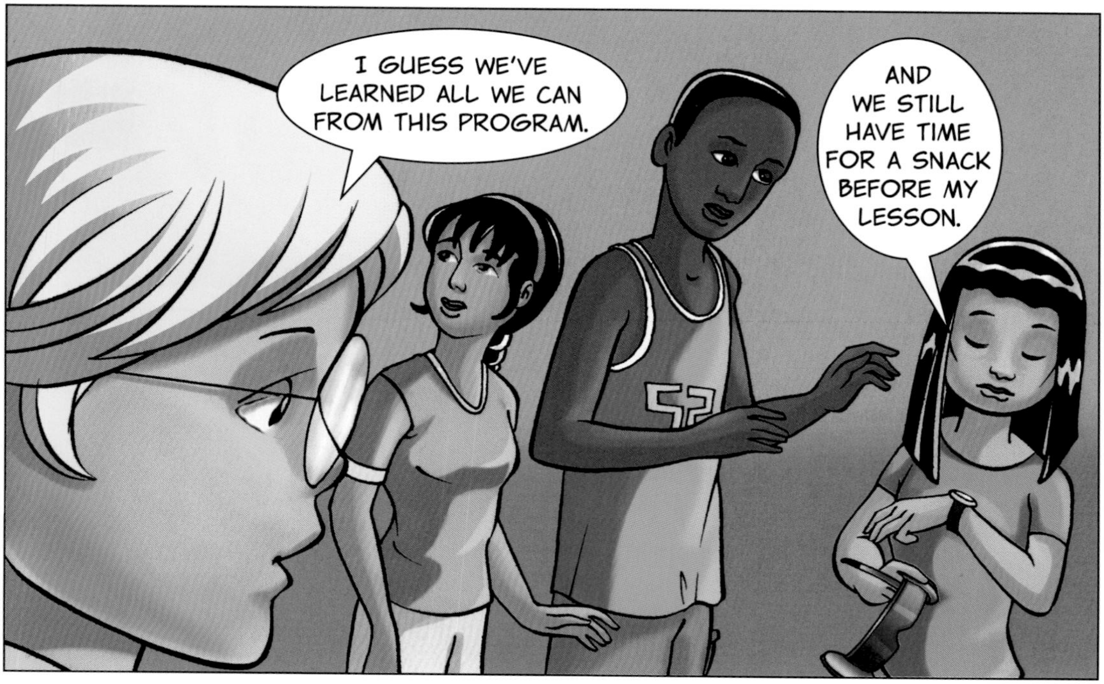
I GUESS WE'VE LEARNED ALL WE CAN FROM THIS PROGRAM.
AND WE STILL HAVE TIME FOR A SNACK BEFORE MY LESSON.

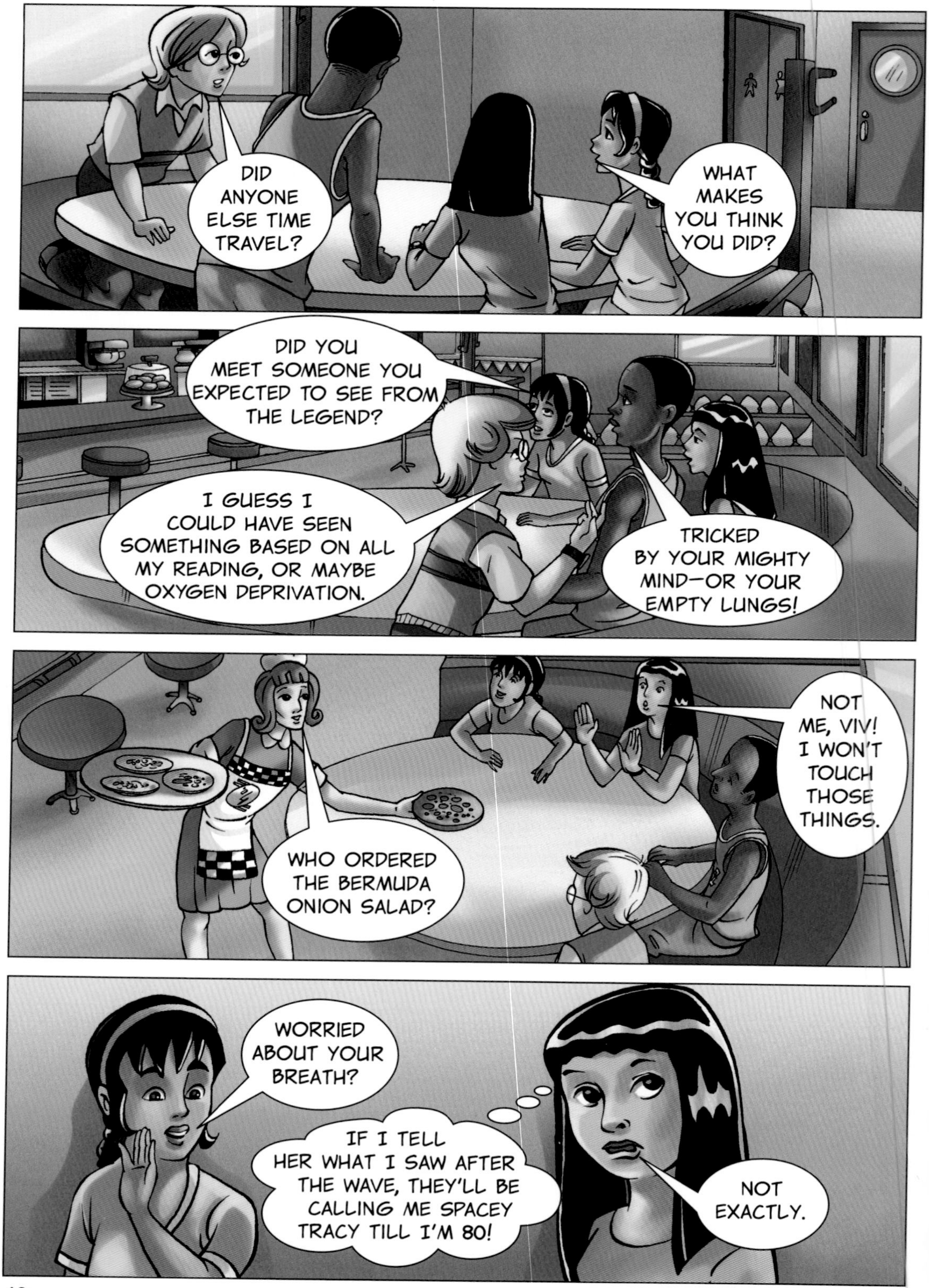

DID ANYONE ELSE TIME TRAVEL?
WHAT MAKES YOU THINK YOU DID?
DID YOU MEET SOMEONE YOU EXPECTED TO SEE FROM THE LEGEND?
I GUESS I COULD HAVE SEEN SOMETHING BASED ON ALL MY READING, OR MAYBE OXYGEN DEPRIVATION.
TRICKED BY YOUR MIGHTY MIND—OR YOUR EMPTY LUNGS!
WHO ORDERED THE BERMUDA ONION SALAD?
NOT ME, VIV! I WON'T TOUCH THOSE THINGS.
WORRIED ABOUT YOUR BREATH?
IF I TELL HER WHAT I SAW AFTER THE WAVE, THEY'LL BE CALLING ME SPACEY TRACY TILL I'M 80!
NOT EXACTLY.

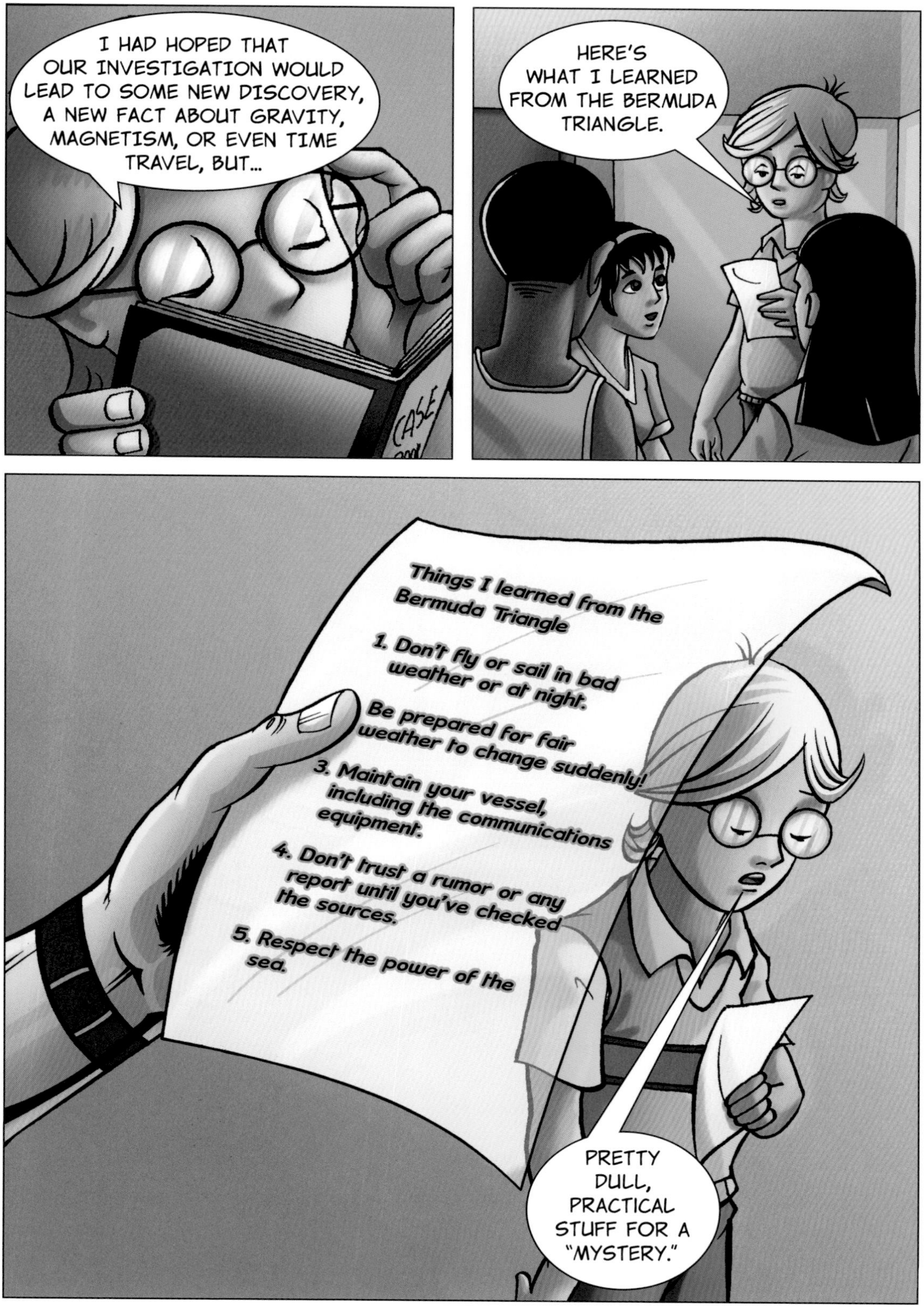
I HAD HOPED THAT OUR INVESTIGATION WOULD LEAD TO SOME NEW DISCOVERY, A NEW FACT ABOUT GRAVITY, MAGNETISM, OR EVEN TIME TRAVEL, BUT...
HERE'S WHAT I LEARNED FROM THE BERMUDA TRIANGLE.
Things I learned from the Bermuda Triangle
1. Don't fly or sail in bad weather or at night.
Be prepared for fair weather to change suddenly!
3. Maintain your vessel, including the communications equipment.
4. Don't trust a rumor or any report until you've checked the sources.
5. Respect the power of the sea.
PRETTY DULL, PRACTICAL STUFF FOR A "MYSTERY."

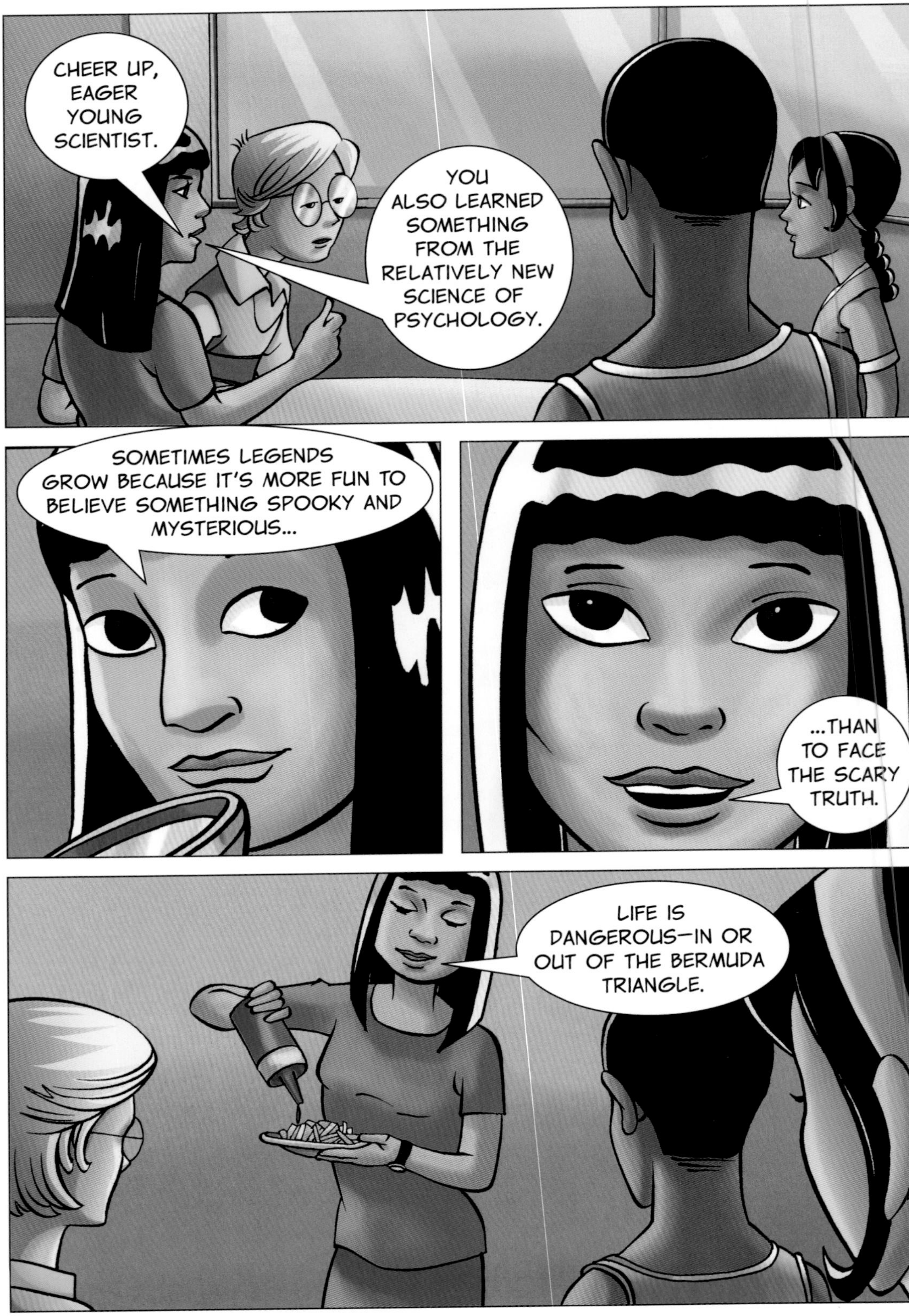
CHEER UP, EAGER YOUNG SCIENTIST.
YOU ALSO LEARNED SOMETHING FROM THE RELATIVELY NEW SCIENCE OF PSYCHOLOGY.
SOMETIMES LEGENDS GROW BECAUSE IT'S MORE FUN TO BELIEVE SOMETHING SPOOKY AND MYSTERIOUS...
...THAN TO FACE THE SCARY TRUTH.
LIFE IS DANGEROUS—IN OR OUT OF THE BERMUDA TRIANGLE.

SO THE MYSTERY OF THE BERMUDA TRIANGLE WAS SOLVED—OR WAS IT?

I'M STILL NOT SURE WHAT'S REAL.

THAT'S A GOOD QUESTION.

RECENTLY, A ROGUE WAVE WAS CAUGHT ON CAMERA FOR THE FIRST TIME. SCIENTISTS NOW KNOW FOR CERTAIN THAT STRONG WINDS, CURRENTS, AND OTHER CONDITIONS CAN CREATE WAVES BIG ENOUGH TO SWALLOW WHOLE SHIPS WITHOUT A TRACE.

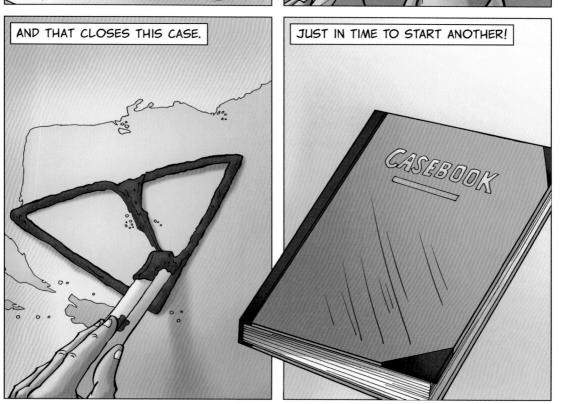

AND THAT CLOSES THIS CASE.

JUST IN TIME TO START ANOTHER!

CASEBOOK

FACT FILE

Bermuda: A group of British islands in the Atlantic Ocean, 677 miles (1,083 kilometers) southeast of New York.

Bermuda onion: A large, mild onion grown in Bermuda and other warm places, often reddish purple and white, and shaped like a flattened sphere.

Coast guard: A group of men and women employed by a government to guard its coasts, prevent smuggling, and help vessels in distress; in the United States, the U.S. Coast Guard.

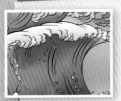

Cowabunga: From 1950s surfer slang, an exclamation of delight and commitment at the start of riding a wave.

FACT FILE

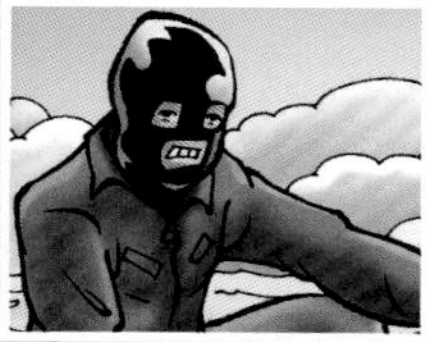

Hijacker: Someone who steals goods in transit by force; someone who violently seizes a vessel.

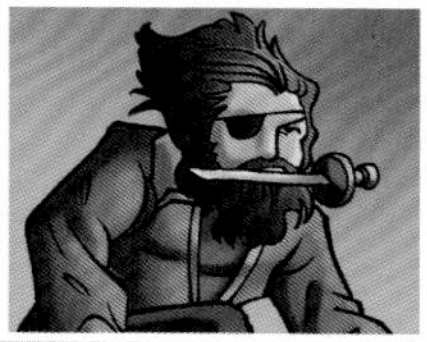

Pirate: (From the Ancient Greek word for "attack") One who robs ships on the high seas; to steal.

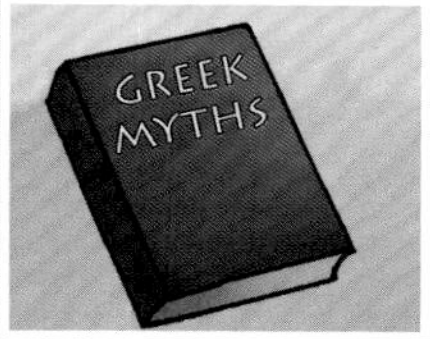
GREEK
MYTHS

Poseidon: The Ancient Greek god of the sea, known to Romans as **Neptune**.

FACT FILE

Rogue wave: A rogue is a vagabond, wanderer, or scoundrel; a fierce, wild animal who wanders apart from the pack. A wave is a curving swell moving along the surface of the sea. A rogue wave is an enormous swell that appears suddenly with potentially disastrous consequences. Once merely a rumor, some said an excuse for poor seamanship, recently proven real.

Shark: (From the Ancient Greek *schurke*, meaning scoundrel*) Any of several large fishes, mostly marine, with a tough, slate gray skin. Most eat fish, but larger sharks will attack people. The shark's **dorsal fin** forms the distinctive triangle visible above the water while it swims. *A shark can also mean a scoundrel who lives by expertly cheating others.

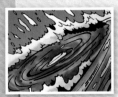

Whirlpool: Violently spinning water which, creates a vacuum at its center, which pulls in floating objects.

Find Out for Yourself

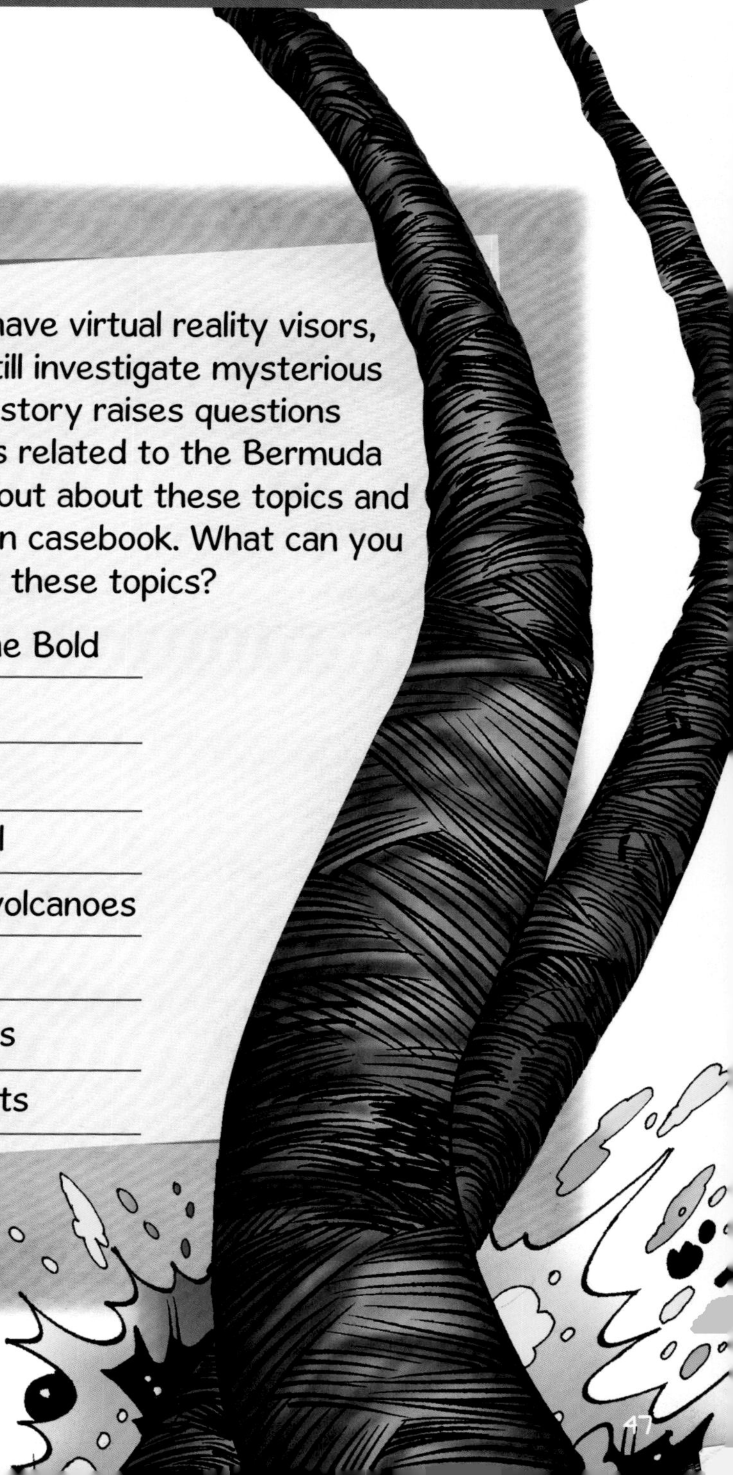

You may not have virtual reality visors, but you can still investigate mysterious matters! This story raises questions about subjects related to the Bermuda Triangle. Find out about these topics and write your own casebook. What can you find out about these topics?

- Brendan the Bold
- Devil's Sea
- Legends
- Time travel
- Undersea volcanoes
- Bill Verity
- Vile vortices
- Waterspouts

Web Sites

To ensure the currency and safety of recommended Internet links, Windmill maintains and updates an online list of sites related to the subject of this book. To access this list of Web sites, please go to **www.windmillbks.com/weblinks** and select this book's title.

About the Author/Artist

Justine and Ron Fontes met at a publishing house in New York City, where he worked for the comic book department and she was an editorial assistant in children's books. Together, they have written over 500 children's books, in every format from board books to historical novels. They live in Maine, where they continue their work in writing and comics and publish a newsletter, *critter news.*

For more great fiction and nonfiction, go to www.windmillbooks.com